PRAISE FOR *POUR ONE FOR THE DEVIL*

"Creepy, atmospheric, and darkly funny, *Pour One for the Devil* has all the trappings of a fine Southern Gothic tale infused with the incomparable wit and dark imaginings of Van Alst. I greatly enjoyed this tale."

—Sonora Taylor, award-winning author of *Little Paranoias: Stories* and *Seeing Things*

"Very cool. Puts me in mind of Machado's *The Resident*."

—Stephen Graham Jones, NYT best-selling author of *My Heart is a Chainsaw* and *The Only Good Indians*

"*Pour One for the Devil* is the first Indigenous Southern Gothic work I've let spill into my soul. Slick and soothing down the hatch, Van Alst's writing will at first burn your tongue, make you curse for being so good, and entice you to slam your glass down and demand another round."

—Shane Hawk, co-editor of *Never Whistle at Night*

"*Pour One for the Devil* is dangerous and delicious, hitting all the right notes. Straightforward at first sip, the story deepens as you take it in, mixing the profane and sacred with a sledgehammer finish. Best keep your wits about you. What should be a simple visit by an academic to a Carolina island historical society becomes a gothic nightmare with a Chicago twist. Another first rate read from Van Alst, who pours himself into the prose, intoxicating and thick with chills."

—Kimberly Davis Basso, author of *Next Door*

"*Pour One for the Devil* dives headlong into all the liquor, lies, and long-simmering moral horrors one could hope for from a Southern Gothic, and finds unique gravity in its lively layering of American atrocity. Van Alst Jr.'s investigator encounters a cinematic swirl of bourbon, blood-soaked soil, and bad magic as he sinks deeper into the eldritch rituals of a sweltering southern island where the Devil is only one of the players, and every last soul is up for grabs."

—Jeremy Robert Johnson, award-winning author
of *The Loop* and *Skullcrack City*

"From page one, Van Alst Jr.'s *Pour One for the Devil* hit all the right notes—a slowly mounting dread, secrets stacked upon secrets, and an ending that at first shocked me and then, after I sat with it a bit, felt inevitable. It's got all the beautiful, heartbreaking touchstones of a truly harrowing gothic tale."

—Keith Rosson, author of *Fever House*

"Rich with legend and lore, Theodore C. Van Alst's *Pour One for the Devil* is a Gothic horror tale in which our sinister home radiates with superstition."

—Cynthia Pelayo, Bram Stoker Award-winning author of *Crime Scene*

POUR ONE FOR THE DEVIL

ALSO BY THEODORE C. VAN ALST, JR.

The Faster Redder Road: The Best UnAmerican Stories of
Stephen Graham Jones (editor)

Sacred Smokes

Sacred City

Never Whistle at Night: An Indigenous Dark Fiction Anthology
(co-editor)

POUR ONE FOR THE DEVIL

A GOTHIC NOVELLA

THEODORE C. VAN ALST, JR.

LANTERNFISH PRESS

PHILADELPHIA

POUR ONE FOR THE DEVIL
Copyright © 2024 by Theodore C. Van Alst, Jr.

Lanternfish Press
P.O. Box 34569
Philadelphia, PA 19101
lanternfishpress.com

Cover Design: Kimberly Glyder
Cover Photograph: Library of Congress, Prints & Photographs Division, HABS, "HABS SC,10-MOUP.V,1-"
Cover Images: Shutterstock/Morphant Creation; New York Public Library

Printed in the United States of America.
27 26 25 24 23   1 2 3 4 5

Library of Congress Control Number: 2022940183
Print ISBN: 978-1-941360-71-2
Digital ISBN: 978-1-941360-72-9

FOR AMIE, EMILY, AND BLUE

S HELLS CRUNCHED UNDERFOOT along the Carolina island
driveway. Off to the right was a small chapel made of
tabby: crushed shells and stone and lime. The chalk white
of dead oysters along its angles caught all the light in the
burnished silver sky. The last strains of the bus's engine
rumbled back toward the causeway as red maple and buck-
eye, live oak and prickly ash drew him into their shade. He
cut his eyes down the humid path, sized more for coaches
than cars, and hummed along with the late afternoon drone
of cicadas and confused crickets. Whips of jade-green grass
and bursting, lanky cattails moved with the aimless breeze;
a pair of shallow canals which shadowed the long lane to the
house burped and croaked with bulgy frogs and dead-eyed
gators. Waterbirds wheeled toward the hot ceiling of sky,
startled by their realization of an unrelenting sun. The smell

of ozone rolled over the land in grey, visible waves. Above the oceanic horizon in the distance sailed lightning-laced, purplewhite thunderheads, eight miles high.

Rounding what he hoped would be the last bend in the lane, he flicked his gaze up to a house that he'd felt before seeing. He was wholly unprepared for the scale of the mansion that glowered back at him. Gables and gablets, red terracotta and hand-hewn cedar shingles, varnished dentil, Doric columns and cypress balconies, a blinding white widow's walk, gaudy corbels and bright-hued brackets, cupolas and brick insets, copper cock, crow, rabbit, and spider weathervanes, planked parapets, and a pair of baleful, glinting picture windows for eyes. It was as if the antebellum architect had incorporated the designs of a century ahead and behind into his scheme and his obviously drunken soul was now paying for his excesses, trapped and glaring through the panes.

He set down his suitcase and scanned the wraparound porch for human life of any kind. He lit a cigarette, took a drag, thumbed the warm lighter in his hand, and struggled to shake the somnolence that pressed in from all sides. There had been a letter. The letter had seemed legitimate enough. He reworked his long black hair into its ponytail holder, wincing as wild strands caught under the strap of his heavy bag. Smoke from the cigarette clenched in his teeth rolled straight up into his squinting eyes.

POUR ONE FOR THE DEVIL

Dear Dr. Van Vierlans–

I have enthusiastically followed your career as a writer of fiction but had been heretofore unaware of your academic work. As such, I read your recent article, "The Coosaw Shell Rings: Ancestral Sites of Power" with great interest. As someone with an abiding interest in history and anthropology, as well as descent from a Sea Island family with deep roots in our ancestral home, I wondered if you might be amenable to providing a reading and discussion of your work here in our humble holdings. We have some rings of our own you might be interested in seeing. We would of course underwrite all expenses, offer a generous honorarium, and be delighted to host you here in our home, which we think would provide for your every desire. We'd be honored if you'd come to a formal dinner Friday evening, and then share your work with our historical society the following afternoon. Please signal your acceptance or regrettable declination via post, at your earliest convenience.

Yours,

Mrs. Elizabeth Morgenstern

Charmed by the genteel approach, more so by the all-expenses paid trip, and thoroughly intrigued by the "generous honorarium" mentioned in the handwritten missive, he confirmed the invitation immediately. His time in graduate school had included a fellowship which paid for him to study Gullah, a West African–based creole spoken in South Carolina and Georgia's Sea Islands, mainly by black folks but (back in the day) quite a few whites also. The language had fascinated him since childhood, and he'd jumped at the chance to finally learn it properly while attending the Gullah Studies Institute through South Carolina State University. Once he landed in Gullah country, he had been thoroughly entranced by Sea Island culture. His master's comprehensives included an examination in the Gullah language, which he passed with highest marks after convincing his advisor it was a creole rather than a "pidgin," as she disdainfully claimed. He looked forward to returning to the area, now as a writer and junior professor.

He knocked the cherry off his smoke, shook out the remaining tobacco onto the ground, shoved the scrunched-up filter in his back pocket to throw away later, grabbed up his suitcase, and headed for the broad front steps. Far-off thunder mocked his trudge up to the gallery where the front entrance waited.

Carved black walnut and leaded glass double doors hinted at amber light within. He scanned the ivory beadboard porch ceiling, expecting paper-wasp nests at least, but there wasn't a spider or cobweb to be seen. Vintage bulbs hung from cast iron fans with beechwood blades that moved the damp air across green and white enameled wood. He didn't hear a single squeak as he walked across the wide planks, which he assumed had been freshly dusted with cornstarch.

He pressed the brass-framed doorbell and the Westminster sequence boomed from somewhere within. Sweating in a charcoal sport coat, white linen oxford shirt, and heavy indigo chinos, he brought his suitcase in front of his body to hide the wet spots, holding onto it with both hands. The strap of his briefcase seared into his shoulder; flies buzzed. Presently, a figure appeared through the window, making their way to answer his brassy summons.

The door opened, and a striking older woman in a traditional black and white domestic worker's dress and apron inquired, "Ebenin', suh. Oonuh hab 'e name?" *Good evening, sir. Do you have your calling card?*

He never remembered to throw business cards in his bag before traveling for lectures and talks, but this was the first time it had caused him any duress. "Ebenin', Auntie. Wid regret, uh don' hab wit' me." *Good evening, Auntie* (a Gullah term of respect). *Regrettably, I do not have one with me.*

She looked him up and down. Tilted her head back, pursed her lips, and said, with squinting eyes and a wicked smile, "Weh fuh oonuh laa'n tuh crack 'e teet?" *Where did you learn to speak?*

He looked her in the eyes ever so briefly, then glanced respectfully down at the threshold, saying, "Frum dem Gullah teechuh Sa'leenuh." *From the Gullah teachers in St. Helena.*

She considered his reply, pushed her tongue out between her front teeth and upper lip, made that sound, and said, "Tek kyuh oonuh se'f—dis house an' dishyuh ooman dain-jus." *Be careful. This house and this woman are dangerous.*

He returned her gaze directly, though fleetingly, and mumbled, casting his eyes downward, "T'engky, Auntie. Uh gwine do de ting f'suttn." *Thank you, Auntie. I'll be sure to do so.*

"All kin' haant dis place," she added, not winking. *There are many spirits around here.*

"Uh yent skay'd." *I'm not afraid*, he offered, laughing nervously, even as he knew her words to be true.

Her smiling face turned toward the floor in thought, but she threw the heavy door wide and ushered him in.

He stepped into the formal parlor and set down his suitcase and valise. The interior matched the cacophonous façade he had seen from the path. Brass, water, and oaken grandfather clocks, verdigrised copper sundials, and golden pocketwatches all set to different times stared at him among Easter-egg-hued Hummel figurines, sprays of bronze and turquoise peacock feathers and duck-grey pussywillows, emerald jade plants and bamboo, verdant bonsai, burgundy velour and aqua velvet club chairs, leather chaises, and tufted ottomans. Layered oriental rugs woven in black, maroon, and sunset yarns coughed seeming centuries of dust when he stepped on them. A Bakelite human-sized automaton with molded black hair on a bulky, squared-off head, with powder-white skin and a charcoal mohair suit, slumped in a vintage Louis XVI round-backed chair, upholstered in garish pumpkin velvet. The lids of the three-dimensional eyes in its otherwise painted-on ivory face softly clicked, though the automaton did not seem to see or hear.

His vision post-orgasmic, he asked if he could smoke inside.

"No, sir," wafted a coastal Carolina lilt from the drawing room. "*That*, we do not do in this home."

"And whom do I have the consummate pleasure of meeting, madame?" he asked, moving into the larger room and looking to charm his way into this dowager's heart with his best top-toothed grin.

"I am the lady of this fine house, Elizabeth Morgenstern. You may call me Miss Lizzie," she offered. Miss Lizzie was high-collared and fine-powdered, blue-grey-coiffured, white-linen-bloused and black-velvet-skirted, looking a lot like Tweety's granny.

"I have previously had the pleasure of meeting—?"

"Auntie Delilah," she finished for him.

"And now yourself," he continued. "I am utterly charmed." Surprisingly, he was.

"Please, sir, do make yourself at home," she rejoined, and he could envision himself doing so.

"Might I place my things elsewhere?" he inquired.

"Your belongings will be attended to by the staff."

"It's no bother, I can bring them along myself."

Miss Lizzie's eyes rolled heavenward, and she involuntarily fanned herself, albeit briefly. "It's best if the ladies attend to that particular task, sir," she said, somewhat sternly.

He recognized his misstep. "Of course. I understand. My apologies, madame."

"But of course. Not a problem whatsoever. You're new to the area."

"Indeed, Miss Lizzie. My ties to the South lie...outside your milieu. But I'm a quick study."

"It's quite all right, Dr. Van Vierlans, I have no doubt you'll acclimate."

"Yes, ma'am."

"Van Vierlans," she murmured. "You have a very interesting name, sir. Not a well-known Dutch name at all," she continued. "It translates to 'Of the Four Spears.' Might that not be its meaning?"

She knew very well its meaning; this was the first question that had revealed something about her true interest in him.

"Well, yes, it is," he declared.

"Might I ask how it came to be your surname?"

"You might, madame, and I might in fact tell you," he smiled. "Perhaps over our dinner?"

"Sounds perfectly delightful, sir," she replied. "We shall reconvene once you are settled. Delilah, please see to it the good doctor's things are brought to the guest room."

Auntie Delilah appeared like sudden mist behind him, near the staircase, holding his baggage.

"Uh gwine tekyuh t'ing tuh de ruhm. Folluh, please." *I'll take your belongings up to your room now. Please follow me*, she said to him, hardly above a whisper.

"T'engky, Auntie," he whispered back, with a glance over his shoulder at Miss Lizzie, who almost imperceptibly rolled her eyes. Yet she made no comment on his knowledge of Gullah.

"Is everything all right?" she half-shouted.

"Yes, ma'am," he said.

Auntie Delilah winked and led him up the stairs.

"ERE'S YUH RUHM, CUZ'N. Oonuh gwin' t'row way dem tuhbackuh butt uh kin smell in dem pocket, o' gwine keep fuh tredjuh?" *Here's your room, cousin. Are you going to dispose of those cigarette butts I can smell in your pockets or are you going to keep them like some kind of cherished possessions?*

"Oh, right," he mumbled. "Uh…" He searched for a trash can.

"Gedduh en gimme dem," she said. "Uh gwin' t'row way downstair." *Grab them up and hand them to me. I'll throw them out for you below.*

"T'engky, Auntie," he mumbled yet again, rummaging in his pockets.

"Dey dey uh bruro fuh dem t'ing. En anudduh blanket

fuh cold," *There's a dresser there for your things and an extra blanket if you get cold.* She pointed him in the right direction. "De Mis lub ankyhall sukkah high buckruh 'ooman, so mek reddy fuh hice plenty drink." *The missus loves the booze just like all these other high-class white ladies, so get ready to drink a lot.*

"T'engky, Auntie. Uh gwine do de t'ing." He handed her the butt from the cigarette he'd smoked on the path up to the house and a couple more from ones that he'd smoked in bathrooms along the bus route, then shoved in his back pocket. He thought to himself that he'd better brush up on his Gullah, if he ever wanted to answer Delilah in any way better than a four-year old.

She vanished the butts into her fist, looked him up and down, and smiled, then turned to go. Silvery traces of ancestors wisped in the wake of the heavy wooden door as she drew it shut behind her.

A s soon as the handle clicked into place, he fell back onto the bed. It had one of those pilled cotton covers—clean, clean white, with small tight tufts in blue, pink, and minty green. It reminded him of his grandma's house. It smelled old and dusty here, but in a scrubbed and mothballed way, very unlike the odor of mouse turds and mildew he'd endured ever since going into academia and starting to rent old country homes where he could do his writing in peace.

He dozed off for what he thought would be a minute or two, boots on and sweating, still wearing his jacket.

It must have been longer than a minute, because he had a couple of those dreams. The kind that might not be merely dreams, might be conjurations or foreknowledge. The ones he could never quite talk about, never wanted to admit to, the fear of owning up to either being a bit too much to bear.

In them were the *haants* of *soldjuhs*, grim and haggard martial faces of both defeat and victory, and *plateyes*, spirits who could freeze you in your tracks, their eyes sudden mirrors in the dark that would pin your feet to the ground. Ghosts who held sway any time after *hag-holluh*, the minutes after midnight, until *crackuhday*, the violet of dawn, right before the moon slid into the coming gold of the morning.

When he struggled awake, he could not move. *De Debble 'ese'f* sat on his paralyzed chest, looking around at the stately architecture, the rich furnishings.

The devil leaned in with tepid breath that smelled of rancid meat and flayed souls and began to whisper stories—starring himself, like always:

Once upon a time, Stella del Mattino made his way through the human streets and alleys of Chicago, full of despair at the way those still gifted with souls treated one another. He looked good in that era—went with the classic modern goatee, $1000 cuts for his jet-black hair, and designer suits—but the *fact that these simple indulgences were available only to a few distressed him sorely. Certainly, those were the few that had made deals and contracts with him in exchange for their immortal souls, but at this juncture he was seriously doubting the worth of said souls. Where was the delight in tormenting those who had savaged and hollowed their own spirits in the pursuit of wealth? What indeed, he thought, was wealth, but the pathological pursuit of...an idea? A perception of betterment, perhaps, or the chance to purchase a place above the rabble?*

Those mummified and delicate classes without substance would break, would crumble at the first tentative torment. Where was the satisfaction in that?

No, the Light Bringer thought. He ached to acquire souls of worth, of value—precisely the ones not usually thought to be possessed of such—those who on this plane accumulated naught of the material but much of the spiritual. He was of course far too old to romanticize the poor, but he did respond to something in them that he could not name, something delectable in their seemingly futile efforts to live and not just survive.

In the pause Van Vierlans, still paralyzed, did his best to ruin the mood with a laugh at Lucifer's silly mandibles, snapping at a thousand miles a second but never connecting, dripping with acidic saliva, longing but never allowed to lunge at his own pulsing carotid. The Morning Star's antennae twitched so fast in fury that they went in and out of focus, while the drool slid further down his billy goat beard.

The two of them stared at each other; time belled out in tiny red clear drips on a Dali clockface. They listened to them fall to the ground together—no other sound lived in the heavy air.

The Devil broke first. "Fine, then. You be the big storyteller. Tell a good one about me, and I'll leave you alone."

"For how long?"

"How long you got?" Satan smirked.

"Forever," Van Vierlans said, unblinking.

"Never say forever. Or never. You'll regret either, trust me."

"Tell you what. If this shit is real, like they say, you leave me be until we meet again after this life is over. If you're a true believer, that is."

"Oh, I believe, all right. To be clear, till *your* life is over, right?"

Van Vierlans sighed, reached for a smoke. "Yeah. Mine."

"Won't be as long as you think it is, son. It's a deal. Deal?" Lucifer stuck out his hand.

"Deal."

They shook on it. The whole signing a contract in blood is bullshit, just so you know. A simple handshake seals any deal with the Devil.

"What's the name of the story?" Lucifer asked.

"Who gives a fuck?"

"I do, man. I need to—"

"What, are you keeping a journal, or something?"

"No. But the title matters." Ol' Nick seemed a li'l hysterical.

"Why?"

"Do you know how many stories there are about me? When I tell it, while me and the boys watch you huddled and weeping on the Plain of Burning Sand, I need it to have a title. How else am I going to point out the significance of what we—"

"How about by sticking it up your ass?"

"You *are* naughty. We're going to have such fun with you." The Devil's eyes flashed.

"Ha. Good luck with that."

"So…title?"

"Black Mariah."

"Oooh. I get a mortal woman? How exciting."

"Keep those pricks in your pants. It's about the card game."

"Well, shit. That's no fun."

"You didn't say it had to be."

"Okay. Whatever. Just don't make me look like an asshole. I get enough of that. You'd be amazed at what people will—"

"Not your therapist, Luce. Just here to tell you a story."

"Fair enough. Get to it, mortal."

"We're gonna stay in Chicago, just so you know. Don't be

scared." He looked Satan in his nearest fluorescent orange eye and took up the thread of the story:

Stella missed his brothers, particularly Azazel; he cared not that they birthed giants, or Nephilim, or whatever these mortal dipshits chose to call his nieces and nephews. He was alone, and lonely, struggling to make his cultured speech understood in the midst of such vulgarity. Doomed to live among these earthly worms, at least for now, having lost a kick-ass hand of poker to the Old Man.

Who the fuck pulls a straight flush over a full house?

G-O-D, that's who, he thought. He must've cheated. And now?

Ten years in this shithole. At least he didn't have to pull this term as an actor like last time. Sure, he made the best of it, taking up as something called a "president" during the Gregorian 1980s, but still. What a drag. He had a good time terrorizing the poor in Nicaragua and invading Grenada, but eating jelly beans and patting Boy Scouts on the head gave him a Prince of Darkness–sized ulcer that he was still getting over.

G-O-D was such a fucking cheater. The guy was the most competitive asshole he had ever known. Sure, Michael was a prick who was all about winning, but at least he had a sense of honor about it. As they blazed down to earth together that one time, intertwined, writhing in the ether (which was a little sexier than Michael liked to talk about), screaming in each other's beautiful faces about how this little war was going to go down, Michael laid out the rules of the game. No backstabbing, no shit-talking, no duplicity–basically all the lofty values that his so-called Christian followers would spit on in the coming centuries, debase for their own devices, and generally shit all over in their ceaseless pursuit of material wealth and gain. Except for the killing part, of course. They seemed to love that. Stella laughed and spread his wings, because he could. Michael bitched and made a face, but Stella tuned him out, because who needs that noise when you're flaming toward a hard landing on Earth?

As he and Michael bounced on the Plains of Meggido, he thought about the coming art the mortals would call film– the movies. He would have to wait until little brother Jesus's 20th century, but damn, he'd be everywhere. There'd be exorcisms and goat gorings and some weird sex, particularly in the English flicks, and he'd even sire a child–but he was most excited about that talented DeNiro guy playing him in the moving theater and making him look pretty good. The musical revival in that century would be just fine as well, with tons of musicians paying him homage. Some silly, but some pretty kick-ass, as they said back then. Those guys in Venom were cool, and Slayer showed commitment, at least in their early years. After the 80s, things got weird, and he couldn't keep up with the developments. He was happy, though, to be in the thoughts of so very many. It seemed things might actually be going his way.

And then, TV. These g-o-ddamned televangelists were every-where. The incessant prayers of heartland hillbillies hissed against his heart and soul. Their supplications had little actual power; they functioned like fast-food versions of home-made love and affection, but each mumbled word was like a needly rain against his black, sooty heart. He longed for the end of his decade in exile and exploded the occasional yuppie on their way home from some office gig that would've crushed their soul in the long run anyway. Stella reckoned he was doing them a favor, really. See? He wasn't all bad.

Anyway, this 20th-century gig wasn't all bad either. He'd learned the latest Italian vernacular while he was here, strolling the neighborhood over on Taylor Street in search of a decent meal, and looked forward to fucking with Dante when he finally got back home tonight. Signore Fiorentino would have a shit fit when Stella whipped out some mod-ern-day peasant dialect on him down in the Eighth Circle. That poseur prick.

The Morning Star strolled down Milwaukee Avenue as dawn's light washed over piss stains and steaming manhole covers, heading for a jaunt downtown on the El. He was going to see a movie to celebrate his final day on the job. One last homeless hand reached up, asking for thirty-seven cents.

This calculated specificity, used to simulate authenticity, pissed him off to no end. He pulled off a shiny and spiffy black wingtip, exposing his razor-sharp hoof, and was ready to end another miserable mortal life when a giant hand reached down from the heavens above the train platform, scooped him up, and set him down in the middle of a hand of seven(hiss)-card stud.

Fuck you, G-O-D.

Fuck you.

When Van Vierlans finished, the Devil looked at him, luminous eyes sheeny with…tears?

"Bitch, are you crying?"

"What? Shut your mouth," Lucifer huffed.

"Hahaha. I got you."

"Did not. It's dusty in here, and you smell like human. You need to clean."

"Sure. Fine. It's okay. We're all a little *human* every now and again. You miss us! And G-O-D is mean to you, too!"

"Speak for yourself. What a disgusting thought."

H E FINALLY WOKE UP in a sweat that he figured to be worth the loss of at least two pounds. Nothing wrong with a little involuntary cardio. The dreams he remembered were far and few between, but whenever Satan visited them, they stuck, even if not in each and every detail.

He wobbled over to the little en-suite bathroom, turned on the cold water tap, and let it run for a full minute, then cupped his hands under the faucet and drank like he'd been forty days in the desert. He glanced in the silvered mirror, reached down again, and splashed two handfuls of cool water onto his face. He grabbed a fluffy white hand towel off the polished pewter rack and ran it over his nose and mouth, breathing deeply of detergent and well-worn cotton.

After that he slow-walked back and forth across the oak-planked floor of the bedroom, pulling out and lighting a cigarette, Miss Lizzie Morgenstern be damned. He waited to exhale till he reached the Palladian windows, though, throwing open the central cast-iron sash and surveying the front grounds of the manse as his cloud of smoke rolled into the still air. Frogs, crickets, humidity, and sundered souls competed for loudest whine over the expansive lawn, which tumbled into sentient woods that splayed unceasingly to the water's edge, where the earth, barely beyond his horizon, faded into the wet, wet breeze.

Dragging deeply on his smoke, he rested his right hand on the edge of the pane, keeping the cigarette outside the sacred perimeter of the house proper. He touched a few fingers to the cool, browned skin of his tattooed right hand—the best skin there is, he mused, and wondered in the same breath what the missus of the house thought of his color, so rare in her world. His mind quickly surmised that this, along with his odd last name and field of study, was exactly why he was here, right now.

Thus far, the old woman was a wonderment. Ghosting through this giant household from another century, oblivious to the changes in the world around her, she maintained standards and mores from a century past. As long as she paid in greenbacks and not greybacks, he didn't much give a shit, at least on the surface. He knew Gullah folks were used to this odd behavior from whites and generally humored them as long as the checks didn't bounce. He recalled a conversation he'd had with an older Gullah man, a semi-pro baseball player who had lived up north in Connecticut but decided to move back to the Sea Islands because, as he declared, "it was easier to live around people you knew hated you for sure." He wanted to spend more time with Auntie Delilah, making the talk, *crack*in *e teet'*, but she appeared to be far busier than he was, he who had already prepared his talk, taken a nap, and squared away his gear. It was probably best not to bother her, he figured.

It left him with time to kill, time to prep up and pray for his best talk, his best words—as he did before every talk, every reading. You never knew who would be in your audience. And in this instance, with Miss Lizzie, at least, guaranteed to be listening, he needed to summon clarity to set some things straight. Though his patron hadn't mentioned it in her letter, he intended to gently disabuse her or any members of her historical society of the notion that Kiawah (the name of a nearby island) and "Kiowa" had any relation whatsoever. People always brought that one up. Thought it meant something. When he'd studied down here previously, he'd heard it from the Institute's museum patrons as well as from fellow students who learned of his Native heritage. But the names of the island and the Great Plains Tribal Nation were no more than a happy coincidence of linguistic indigeneity.

Coosaw Island did indeed have shell rings, though they required further investigation as anomalies to the area. But they lent her no power, much as she seemed to want them to. He thought back to one of the stories Satan had licked into his ear, a tale of some Confederate soldiers forced into cannibalism, but it seemed so fucking cliché he figured the Prince of Lies had been bored and having fun with him. That was the fuzzy foggy shit he needed to dispel from his brain if he was to land a fish like Miss Lizzie, someone who could endow a chair or hand him a huge spend-down account which could pay for years of research and travel— the biscuits and gravy, the cornbread and beans, of his trade.

The room was so large he hadn't given a second thought to the bank of windows arrayed along the north side of his quarters. Turning from the now open-to-the-water Palladians, he walked over to the curtained glass, pulled back the gauze-lined lace drapery, and found himself facing a small veranda framed by French doors. He opened them and stepped out onto the harlequin-terrazoed limestone, appreciated the tiled table and mosaic-inlaid chairs and the thoughtfulness of the potted flowers, even though he couldn't stand geraniums. He placed his hands on the carved stone rail that curved along the half-circle of the balcony, lifted his face into the air, and breathed deeply. The familiar pose and the smell of salt air took him back to the roll of the red-lit catwalk he'd once ridden on the aircraft carrier where he was stationed in the luminous cerulean of the eastern Mediterranean—off the coast of Beirut, during the war and eventual bombing of the airport. He remembered when the helicopters brought the bodies to the aircraft carrier after the bombing, how some of the sailors and marines had been taken so suddenly from this world that their spirits only now realized their freedom and visibly fled the body bags in the holds of the thundering Sea Knights that rushed toward the carrier, the freezers of which had been emptied of their stores in order to make way for the hundreds of dead who could not be held onshore in the morgue-less heat of autumn Lebanon. He watched the spirits twist into the ether, envied their escape.

He ought to mention this story tonight in his warm-up for tomorrow's lecture, he thought. The old woman might appreciate his military service the way they do in the South, and open that fat checkbook even wider. He wondered for a brief moment at his moral base or lack thereof. And lit another smoke.

MISS LIZZIE was a formidable woman. As a Northerner, he was intrigued of course by her anachronistic authority over the household and the plantation mentality she alone in the manor maintained in the face of the 20th century, though her stentorian voice and absolute confidence in her employees' belief in the same appeared to be a source of amusement to them. That was a fine thing, he knew. The knowing resilience of the house staff was reassuring. But the Tweety's-grandma vibe was deep in the ambience of the estate, and he vowed to dig deeper into its source.

Refreshed and resolute, he wandered down the white-walled hallway, finding his way to the kitchen by way of a back stairwell, which appeared to have been little used as of late. A fine duvet of dust skirled around his feet a hair above the gleaming, dark wood planks, which caught the claret and golden glow of the drowning sun as it streamed through the stained-glass window at the end of the hall, illuminating some passionate torture of Jesus on his way to Mount Calvary as well as the path to the kitchen.

"GOOD EVENING," he beamed, alighting from the last step into the voluminous kitchen. Hanging copper-bottomed pots and pans, along with every possible cooking utensil rendered in stainless steel, swayed amid steam and a light breeze from an open window somewhere beyond his immediate vision. Windows lined a white-bricked wall above cupboards and countertops stacked with heaps of sparkling-clean, heavy, bone-colored dishes and bowls. A massive granite counter topped a central island laden with clear-eyed fresh fish, iced seafood, and outrageously colored fruits and vegetables he'd never seen before. Gold-brown-crusted fruit and nut pies and pastel cakes in lime, blush, and baby blue cooled on racks. His inner-city eyes buzzed at the bounty before him. Even in the Ivy League he'd never seen such organic bounty and beauty available in any kind of setting, much less what he thought of as a country galley—but he'd seen the humblest kitchens become elegant dining halls when filled with aunties and uncles and cousins, grandmas, grandpas, brothers and sisters, mas and dads.

Delilah watched his face closely and said, "Here's the cousin I told you about. He talks Gullah like a little boy, but at least he tries."

Her two younger colleagues, dressed in soft, warm-colored calico dresses and white aprons, hooted big. One chuckled, "Ebenin', cuz'n." The other added, "Welcome to Gullah country." They appeared to be twins, though one of the women could be distinguished from the other by a long, shiny scar that snaked up her arm from wrist to elbow.

"T'engky, Aunties," he said.

Delilah smiled. "See? Uh tol' you so. He doesn't have enough words yet. Cousin, you want to switch to de buckruh talk?" (*White man's language.*)

"I'll try to make the talk, Auntie. Unless it bex oonuh so," he offered. (*Unless it bothers you too much.*)

"We'll make de buckruh talk for a bit, mix in the real talk maybe. You'll learn again."

"Please tell me more about this house—about Miss Lizzie, if you don't mind," he said.

"What do you want to know?" asked Beryl.

"Which first?" asked Pearl.

"How come?" asked Delilah.

"I'm curious. I'm a professor, a teacher. It's my job to wonder about things."

"Wondering can get you into trouble, cousin," Delilah said.

"Fuh true," he replied, "but uh cain't he'p mese'f."

"Nemmine alltwo dese 'ooman," Pearl shushed. *Never mind these two women.* "Fus' gwinin' off dishyuh plantesshun widdem oshtuh shell eb'ryweh duh cut 'e foot staa't dem crazy min' duh Majuh Morgenstern." *In the beginning, this plantation with the oyster shells that will cut your feet wherever you go first started with a vision in the mind of Major Morgenstern.* "He was an officer in the first war against the Redcoats," she said, switching to English.

"Miss Lizzie's ancestor fought in the Revolutionary War?"

"That's right. They gave him this whole island after the Battle of King's Mountain. He was some kind of a hero there, they say. Didn't make much sense to me." Her brow creased. "Especially since all kinds of Native folks still lived here at the time. But this Colonel Campbell who gave him the land paid no mind to the fact. You know, those folks around here were probably your cousins or something. My grandmama told me some of their words and they sounded a lot like the ones you were praying in your sleep."

What the hell? he thought. Either the antebellum walls were thinner than he thought, or she'd been hanging around outside his door while he took a nap. Either way...

His mind raced through the Siouan-speaking peoples of the area: Catawba, Waccamaw, Cheraw, Pee Dee. His heart registered the loss of so many relatives. Beryl caught the look it made in his eyes.

"Go on, Pearl," she said, red-and-white-striped towel in hand, furiously drying a dish.

Delilah made that sound with her teeth again. "Tell it," she nodded.

"Anyway, the major made himself a plan, even though folks told him the dirt was no good. The land was sandy and hilly, sometimes rocky, but the major, he got educated on some things by masters from out here in the islands who he met up with during the war. He learned how rice beat the pants off cotton even then, even off tobacco."

This he knew to be true with absolute certainty. He had visited the cemeteries in Charleston, had seen the extravagant mausoleums of the rice planters, raised his eyebrows at the Union Jacks decorating graves on Memorial Day.

Pearl continued from low in her throat, with tears in her voice. "He went and stole our ancestors, the greatest farmers the world has ever known."

As the room went solemn, he thought about what an understatement that was. First the British, then the Americans kidnapped and enslaved the best and brightest of West Africa's coastal and upcountry farmers throughout the 18th and 19th centuries, forcing them to apply their agricultural genius to a dozen varieties of rice across the many topographies of their stolen lands. Few people knew this fact, and even fewer knew their descendants were still here today—full of memories and a culture and language most whites would never know. But back in the day these lands were full of malaria and particularly hostile to white planters, who only spent a month or two on the islands every year. Thus, the folks who would form the Gullah culture were left to their own devices most of the time, and their social, cultural, and linguistic structures survived even today. He knew himself fortunate to hear them share their stories.

"I can tell you about the house." Beryl shifted the mood and snapped them all back to the present day. "Our grandfather a few generations back was the main builder."

"That would be wonderful, cousin."

"No expense was spared. The Morgensterns were rice people—rich people. All the crazy stuff in this house came straight out of their old country. Clocks and tapestries, tiles, even the wood for the panel walls. Half the garden back there is tulip bulbs straight from Holland. They told Grandpa to make it pretty, make it like it was going to be his own."

Pearl cut in: "They made like they was Mason fuh true, but same lukkuh ancien' 'gyptian Mason, too. Gramma would tell us kids they had buried a boy who had been born foolish right in the cornerstone like olden times. I thought it was to keep us scared and quiet, but some nights the wind whines even when the leaves don't move at all."

"Gran'puh tol' us dat, too," said Beryl.

"Yup. Maum Nenge too," added Delilah. "Ceppin' 'e tol' me 'e had a secret hatch, dat 'e could go out at night, 'trech 'e leg when he got cramp up in dey. 'E say e likkuh sweet t'ing, paw dem crooky han' 'roun' de kitchen, look fuh dem sugar cube, ebenso stan' fron' de fridgedator and swill dem sweettea fuhm de pitchuh in de black of night, 'e plateye shinin' in de moonlight frum de winder."

"Uh nebbuh yeddy sukka t'ing," said Beryl.

"Uh membuh dat, uh t'ink," Pearl replied. "O' mebbe dream de t'ing…"

She stared down at the floor. He stared down too, wanting a cigarette at the same time as he wanted nothing more than a hug, or to rub and warm his own arms, at the least.

He pulled his long ponytail around to the front, fiddled with the end, and announced he was headed out back for a smoke.

"Keep a watch fuh dem dog," advised Auntie Delilah, low and solemn. She glanced up and out the window over the kitchen's great soapstone sink, tracing the last embers of the dying day, and said in English: "Ol' King even might be out there huntin' around."

Beryl and Pearl laughed. "Stop it—don't tease," they said.

"Whaaaaat?" Delilah smiled, switched back to Gullah. "Oonuh don' know. Dem dog alltime sniffin' roun'."

"Ain't no dog dey." Pearl frowned.

"Cu'd be, do'," Beryl countered. "Bin plenny year since, but no one need tek dat risk."

Delilah chuckled. "Bek tuh wu'k. We gots a suppuh fuh make. Cuz'n gwine nyam gud t'night, 'e hab shaa'k wid 'e swimp an' grit. Mebbe cootuh soup, too. An' de missus wan' lobstuh t'ermidor tonight. Dat gwine be de wu'k dey."

Their laughter echoed in his ears like the buzz from sweet blush wine. He kept one hand on the cypress railing and his eyes on his boots making their way down the wide, silvered back stairs, which led to a flagstone patio and tropical gardens. He laughed to himself at what they didn't know—that his dog medicine would save him from any strays wandering the woods—and hopped off the last tread onto the blue and grey slate pavers, mortared with fine white sand. He reached into his blazer pocket and pulled out his smokes, fishing one from the yellow pack with the red and black Indianhead logo, sticking it in the corner of his mouth, and lighting it with a weathered zippo embossed with a US Navy anchor—the Chief Petty Officer's symbol of rank, welded on for effect and easy sales. It was the last thing his Pop had ever given him. Finding the flints and the naphtha to keep it working was a pain in the ass, but that wasn't shit compared to what the old man was probably dealing with, gone from this world fifteen or so years now. He had tried to talk him back into traditional ways, but Pops was stubborn and went out as a Christian. Probably still trying to cross over, he figured, and shuddered.

He strolled through a riot of flowering plants and shrubs he had no hope of naming, though quite a few appeared to be giant versions of houseplants he saw in the grocery store floral section back home. The pinks, blues, and magentas hummed, like a celestial photographer had cranked up the saturation and seriously fucked with the hue and tone, rendering the light pastel and warm like in a hotel-sale oil painting that you know is terrible. But still, you look at the illumination and wonder, *How did they do that?* Scents of vanilla and rose fought with nutmeg and cardamom. He looked down his smoking arm to see his skin popping glossy with the humidity; the tattooed reds, greens, and sky-blues on his hand glowed in the magic light, which flowed as a burnt gold mist over the deep pine treeline.

Van Vierlans grinned at his good mood and fortune, counted himself luckier than he'd ever thought he'd be, and sat on a handily placed marble bench. A slightly too-warm breeze laden with the early promise of night-blooming jasmine loosened his dark hair from its hammered silver band, and he lowered his head, shaking it gently with a secret smile. Fortune this good, he knew, came to folks like him about once every three generations, and he was glad to be at the head of the line this time around.

He flicked the cherry off his smoke, rolled the tobacco out onto the ground, and shoved the butt into his pocket before strolling back to the house.

He took the stairs two at a time, resting his hand on the smooth brass knob of the back-porch door before he went in. Inside, the cousins were speaking in hushed voices, which was odd for them. He listened for a half-minute or so, but the muted Gullah was beyond his ability, so he opened the door slow and wide, giving them time to adjust into whatever voice it was they wanted to present to him. They smiled almost in unison at his return, only Beryl hesitating before turning on the shine. She spoke first.

"My sisters ain't told you 'bout the Mistuh. Oonuh prolly want to know 'bout him." She emphasized the last word.

"I'm happy to hear about whatever you want to tell me, cousin."

"Mmhmm," mused Delilah.

Pearl said, "or 'bout de Missus."

"Eeduh. Don' mek me no nebbuhmin'," he threw in.

"Okay, cousin," Beryl sighed. "'Ere we go, den. Mistuh Morgenstern, 'e still here. 'E on de groun'. 'E lib de chu'ch."

"What?" he asked, thinking perhaps he'd misunderstood.

"Dat's right. De chu'ch oonuh see on de way? Mek from tabby on de righthand side? 'E duh chain up dey," Delilah cut in. "Yuh, on'y t'ing not duh chain roun' heah dem dog."

"What do you mean? He's still alive?"

"Fuh true," Beryl nodded.

"'E duh chain up dey," Pearl confirmed.

He leaned back on the granite counter with both hands. Puffed away a few stray hairs. Played back that "Angie Baby" song in his head. This Southern Gothic shit was a lot.

"The ol' man? *The major?* A haa'nt?" he asked.

"No suh. De husband Miss Lizzie," Beryl said.

"Huccome? That's crazy."

"'E duh man full'up wid bex," Delilah said. "'E wan' divorce. But Miss Lizzie 'tronguh." She switched to English so he could keep up. "Mister Peter retreated into his own mind. Busied himself with his automatons, his books. Had no time or lost interest for more…earthly matters. He thought he'd do Miss Elizabeth a favor and ask for a divorce, but she wasn't having it; a divorce was unacceptable, regardless of the…*unusual* circumstances of their marriage."

There's no way this is true, he told himself. I'm trapped

in some bullshit kitchen story these three tell themselves to pass the time.

"We got maybe ten minutes 'til supper," he said. "Perhaps we can talk more about this later."

"We can talk about this whenever you want, cousin. Time is something we got plenty of," Beryl replied.

"Bes' be ready. 'E duh hab' de tremble all de day long," Delilah warned. When he didn't respond right away, she switched to English. "I hope you're prepared. She's had the shakes all day. The need for drink has taken over her life."

"No, no. Uh yeddy fine. Uh jis'—" *No, I hear and understand. I just–*

"So you best be on your toes, cousin."

"Uh brung much hebby belly fuh drink, Auntie. Now uh gwin' needum."

"I hope you did, cousin. You don't know drinking until you spend an evening with Miss Lizzie."

He rolled his eyes heavenward, thought, Shiiiiiiiit, we'll see about that.

M ISS LIZZIE sat at the head of a long, white-linen-covered dinner table, its turned mahogany legs peeking out from under the lush drapery. Service for two, salad forks, dessert spoons, and water and wine glasses winked in the electric chandelier's glow and the abundant candlelight. Her frosted highball glass slowly sweated into the pale tablecloth's weave; with an excited imagination after hearing the stories of the cousins, he couldn't help seeing tears in its clear rivulets—four hundred years of unheard tears, shed by the women who kept this house.

The lady herself wore a black velveteen waistcoat, a voluminous pleated skirt, and a starched, white, board-collared cotton blouse that was cinched at the neck with a cameo brooch of some severe ancestor in profile. Someone who had watched over things with prescient foreboding and pensive judgment, no doubt. A wall of books—some leather-bound, others painted, all of them dusty—filled the frame behind her. He reached back and flipped his ponytail. She picked up her tall glass, drank deeply, and arched an eyebrow, watching him over the rim. He adjusted his chair and, compelled by the setting, flicked the imaginary tails on a coat he didn't have; his cheap blazer was trying its best. He cleared his throat and smiled, returned her gaze briefly.

She spoke first. "Tell me about what and why you write. It's such an unusual choice for someone of your...heritage. As I understand it, you might be predisposed to the oral tradition. That would be more in keeping with tradition, would it not? Telling tales to historical societies and museum crowds, rather than scribbling books and articles."

He shrugged off the offensive comments, a thing he had long practice in. "Every story of mine is post-apocalyptic literature. It says, here we are, finding our way home to each other through the holocaust."

"I don't follow," she said.

"I mean that writing is resistance. It's particularly effective when done, and done well, in the enemy's language."

"Is that how you see me, then? As an enemy?"

"You're certainly not an invited guest." He suppressed a grin.

"I was born here through no fault of my own," she parried.

So, she wanted to fence. Very well, he would advance. "But your ancestors invaded, did the things they did, and now you reap the benefit."

She slashed at the accusation. "Would you have me simply up and abandon all this? These lands, my charges, my ladies of the household?"

"I'm quite certain things would work out, were you to undertake such a bold and noble move, madame."

Her face moved in ways that made her seem to be actually considering his words, though all the while she was looking him deep in the eyes, too searingly and too long for his liking. She drained her highball, tipping way, way back to do so, letting the ice rest on her lined and pinched mouth before lowering it and slamming it on the table. She laughed sharply, the way wolves do right before they eat. She rang a small, ebony-handled brass bell at her right hand and waited for the drink that would always shortly appear in the hand of her kind.

D ELILAH ARRIVED a minute or so later carrying a fresh glass on a sterling serving tray, the just-cut lime wedge so sharp and lush he could smell it over the gin and tonic as she walked up behind him. She set the cocktail down on a linen doily then stood off to the side, near to but not leaning on a gleaming walnut highboy. Miss Lizzie raised her glass.

"Are you falling behind, sir? I feel as if I'm drinking alone; you've hardly touched your glass at all. I thought your people…" she trailed off. "Forgive me," she finally said. "I meant no offense."

He took the insult, as he had all the others, and chewed the inside of his lower lip. "No, no. My apologies," he managed after a couple of seconds. Then he downed the entirety of his scotch on the rocks, melted cubes and all.

She smiled wide enough to show a couple of premolars. "Another, Doctor?"

"Certainly," he replied.

Delilah grabbed his glass and headed toward the kitchen, performing the duty she had already assumed would be shortly required. Madame was on a roll.

A FTER DELILAH'S DELIVERY of his second drink, she resumed her station to his right and Miss Lizzie's left. She folded her hands in front of her and stared off into her own world, leaving one ear cocked to this one.

The Lady Morgenstern drained off half her glass and asked, "Do you know why I invited you here?"

"Madame, if I did, I might not have come. It's inquiry and intrigue, after all, that keep life interesting."

"I do like you, you know." She smiled.

"I do know." He beamed back. "If you did not, this visit would likely have been over before it started."

"I appreciate your humility, Doctor, though it is not required as a condition of your honorarium."

"I didn't think it would be, Miss Lizzie. After all, the last people who at least have pretentions to be chivalrous folks in this country are planted 'round here somewhere, if I'm not mistaken. Of your honor I had no doubt."

"I thought you were from the North, sir. Your manners are impeccable, and largely unexpected."

"The North surrounded us, madame. We maintained our manners in the face of their…presence."

"You must be even now a sight more tolerable than we are, sir."

"We *must*, as you point out."

"Unfortunately, yes," she countered. "This business of 'we,' I would like to discuss, Doctor, if you don't mind."

"I'm not sure why I might object, madame. Please continue."

"You and I would appear to share a Dutch heritage," she said.

"It would appear so."

"But there is more to it, isn't there?"

"How do you mean, ma'am?"

"Come now. You are a Four Lance by blood, or heritage, or whatnot. Why translate the surname into Dutch?"

"It means the same thing, does it not?" he asked.

"True, but why Dutch?"

"Why, to honor those ancestors, madame."

"Which ones?"

"All of them, of course."

"How are they *all* honored, when you eliminate the Native...sensibility, from your surname?"

"If you must know, I'm actually a Van Wees—my great-grandfather was an orphan in the Netherlands, heritage unknown. After arriving here and marrying into a Native family, he changed his last name to reflect his newfound kinship with his wife's family. That aside, Madame, have you considered the difficulty with which one might move through life with the English version of that surname, here in the United States?"

"I had not."

"The American context predisposes to certain preconceived notions about the carrier of such an aristocratic name, does it not? And I have found that, though they profess an accepting embrace of what they term 'diversity,' the majority of academics are possessed of little actual open-mindedness when it comes to heritage. Therefore,

I honor not just my lone discoverable Dutch ancestor by using that tongue in my surname—but all of my Indigenous ancestors by passing unnoticed through academia until I am in halls and classrooms where none might complain of my presence. Rest assured, madame, my ancestors and family know exactly who I am and what I am about."

"*Proost*," she said, raising and draining the rest of her glass.

Auntie Delilah caught his eye and winked.

"I HAD HOPED you might tell us about the people of this area, the Native people of this area, and in particular about the power of the stone circles found in the Sea Islands," Miss Lizzie continued after a few minutes of silence that he thoroughly enjoyed. "Those are a lot like your shell rings, are they not?"

"Not necessarily. And only the Native folks, Miss Lizzie? I could likely tell you a thing or two about the Gullah folks as well as the planters."

"That won't be necessary, Doctor. As president of the historical society, I am interested in the stone circles, which I believe are versions of your shell rings. I am well versed enough in those other stories."

"Well, madame, perhaps one side of the story—"

"As I said, Doctor, I am not interested in those stories. Those stories are not why you are here."

"They might be, considering my own interests, but that would seem to be for another conversation."

"Indeed, Dr. *Van Vierlans*, indeed."

A NOTHER ROUND OF COCKTAILS, accompanied by a survey of the recent weather and the effects of extreme humidity on human hair, ended in an uncomfortable silence that finally prompted Van Vierlans to say: "It's interesting to me that you would focus your inquiry, Miss Lizzie, on the nebulous and likely imaginary power of the stone circles. Perhaps I've spent too much time in the North." He smiled. "Where people are not predisposed to give credence to matters of the spirit, or worlds they have no material grasp of."

Auntie Delilah leaned in from her station by the high-boy and quietly offered, "Dem people dey dey nussuh mannusuble."

"Fuh true, Auntie," he agreed.

Miss Lizzie rolled her eyes up and to the left, translating, then shot back, "I do find them somewhat rude, but I wouldn't say they have *no* manners."

"It depends entirely upon one's place in their world, as it were," he offered. "The denizens of what is known as the Ivy League occupy a world of their own making, and rare is the day when they allow the entry of any not bred to their caste."

"I am not entirely unfamiliar with this league of which you speak," she replied. "My own father, Peter Morgenstern, is an alumnus of Princeton."

This was news to Van Vierlans; his investigation of her family prior to his acceptance of her invitation had not turned up this information, though he did remember reading that her husband was an alumnus.

"Do tell, Miss Lizzie. I am endlessly fascinated by the schools that the Ivy League endowments operate as seeming side interests."

"Oh, yes. Princeton is and has been the destination of our best and brightest here in the Old Confederacy. And before you tell me how Yale was the one northern school that did not return students during the War Between the States, preferring to keep their students in residence and dialogue, surely you are also aware of Freetown in New Jersey. Surely you know of the neighborhood of freed slaves."

He did. "Of course, Miss Lizzie. That neighborhood is called Witherspoon, and is a place settled by freedmen prior to the establishment of the university itself. Indeed, it provides a particular atmosphere to Princeton not found elsewhere."

He had visited Princeton once. In fact, it was the site of the first paper he'd presented in graduate school. What had struck him most profoundly were strange imbalances in the local demographics. He did not encounter a single student or youth of student age working in any of the pizzerias or other dining establishments. Instead, there seemed to be an improbable abundance of middle-aged, matronly types, seemingly bussed in from Jersey burbs or ex-urbs, all named Joan, or Marie, or something vaguely ethnic. The lack of youthfulness and melanin was at best disturbing for an otherwise nondescript college town.

He mentioned it to the party he was traveling with. None of them found it odd in the least.

He still thought about that moment, about the utter lack of awareness that afflicted the majority of his colleagues, who would probably never truly consider, much less understand, the disparities that affected him near daily. It was less a weird world than a shitty one, he decided.

Delilah broke in, deciding Miss Lizzie had had enough to drink to inaugurate the point in the evening where protocol was set aside. "Miss Lizzie, perhaps you could tell the doctor about the mister's automatons."

Miss Lizzie managed to look annoyed and as if she had seen a ghost at the same time—an estimable twist of face, he thought to himself.

"Auntie Delilah. I think this is neither the time nor the place for such—"

"What? Idiosyncrasies? Secrets that might find empathy, or at least understanding?"

Van Vierlans watched Delilah. She was leaning, two-handed, on the table, massaging the lace textures of the ivory tablecloth with a slow and methodical rhythm, staring intently at her employer. She continued, "What, Missus? We yent gwine taa'k 'bout dem robot? Dem 'bominashun de maussuh mek? Dey duh hol' fas dem soul duh Gullah fo'k?"

He considered this. Apparently, Miss Lizzie's Princeton-educated father had built some sort of robots back in the day, an obsession he'd brought home along with his degree. The house had been full of them at one time, but the last known one resided in the parlor upon its cushions of pumpkin velvet. Delilah believed these creations were powered by the imprisoned spirits of her relatives. They had been arguing about it for years, it seemed. Christ on the Cross, what the hell was happening here?

"Papa only filled a need, something this house required in order to function in a proper manner," Miss Lizzie hissed, lips pursed and pinched. "You people refused to...*attend to* certain spaces around here."

"Dey duh haa'nt, Missus. We cyan' go dey. Oonuh know dat fuh true!"

"And why not, Delilah? Why do you insist that they are haunted? Apart from primitive superstition, there was and is no reason you cannot move through any place in this house or on its grounds that you might wish. But no. Your irrational fears left my father with no choice but to seek a way to compensate for your childishness."

Delilah's face hardened. She thinned her lips, switched to the American tongue. "Our prudent reverence for our ancestors, which you refer to as 'childishness,' is naught compared to the murderousness of *your* people, or to their lack of respect."

She must be pissed, he thought. The hard edge in her voice was a novel addition to the conversations he had heretofore experienced in this…god*damned* house. He felt the sweat pop under his jacket, even as he kept his gaze on her face.

"Why did you invite this man to our home?" Delilah continued. "You say you're interested in his work, but it's my estimation you're after something else. Haven't I told you those stone circles you're so interested in aren't going to bring back your son, any more than they can set free the father you call husband from his madness? Rocks don't have that power—they're just repositories of your projected desires. There's no magic in the world like unto what you're looking for."

Delilah's calm was deeply unsettling. He said fuck it and lit a cigarette. Miss Lizzie stared at him coolly but didn't mention the smoke. She turned her gaze back to Delilah:

"I'd have you explain yourself, missy. Do tell what you *think* you know."

Delilah began to describe a scene which brought back to him the nightmares he had fought through earlier in the afternoon. She pulled him through time with her to the 1900s. Her melodic voice painted the house as a place reanimated with gaudy flocked-gold, burgundy, and emerald wallpaper. Gullah language glistened and rolled throughout the rooms, its musical tones reassuring him, centering his presence in this dimension. He caught his bearings, peered down in mild surprise at his tailed pearl waistcoat, lemon linen shirt, and dark wine cravat. In his right hand was a carved meerschaum pipe, which he put to his lips and puffed on, then froze in place as chalk-white, square-headed automatons with drawn-on faces glided silently through the halls carrying laundry or trays of iced tea.

He shuddered, rubbed his arms. Delilah's voice brought him back—

"Missus, oonuh know dat duh folks fum 'ere wuh killt by yuh fambly. Oonuh cyan' lie 'bout dat."

"Delilah, I'd have you speak English," Miss Lizzie demanded, her words beginning to slur.

"Have it your way, Elizabeth," Delilah answered, "cause then there'll be no mistaking. You know how many of the local people were killed by your family and you can't lie about it. You've been toting that guilt on their behalf for multiple generations. Bringing this man here will do nothing to assuage your remorse. Nor will it free the souls of any of your ancestors or their victims, no matter what he knows."

"I believe he knows more than either of us thinks he might," said Miss Lizzie.

He tried to process this, listing to either side as his moorings loosened.

"Do not put your shame, nor your guilt, upon this man," Delilah commanded.

Other voices crowded him. He could hear them, faintly as if they came from a farther shore, and pick out some of the words—they were prayers in a Siouan language. *Tunkasila. Unsimalayo. Wocikiye...wocikiye. Omakiyayo... Wopila tanka tunkasila...unsimalayo...* They mixed with words from another language that he didn't understand at all, even if he felt the meaning, a language that sounded like Mvskoke. They rose in an individuated chorus of men, women, and children, their plaintive supplications rising up through the argument taking place at the table. So many relatives in such pain.

He held his hands up to the sides of his head. So much for visiting a quaint southern mansion and lecturing to an elderly historical society.

"You are outrageous," Miss Lizzie accused, her voice rising.

"The only outrageous thing here, madame, is your memory, or lack thereof," Delilah countered.

Pearl and Beryl edged their way into the room, eyes intent upon Miss Lizzie, who felt the pressure of bodily presence coming from the kitchen and whipped her head around, sneering:

"What do you two want? I suppose you're here to support your sister."

"What do we want? Justice, I suppose," said Pearl.

"That would be good," Beryl added, picking up on the mood in the room. "Along with your ass in a sling."

"Yes. Justice. How about some justice, sisters?" Delilah asked.

"Yeah. That would be good," they replied in unison.

Delilah turned to Van Vierlans. "Elizabeth Morgenstern is something else, something not of this world. In all my years, I've never encountered such savagery. Keeping us in these uniforms and this world of her making, regardless of what the clocks in the outside world say the year is—that's part of it. But her man out in the church says a whole lot more."

Miss Lizzie stood up, surveyed the room, met each of their glances in turn, and then held up her manicured hand, ripe with bright jewelry. One filigreed gold ring in particular, set with a massive plum stone, caught the chandelier's light as she strode into the kitchen. Her black velveteen petticoat bustled through the double-hinged door and glided almost instantly back out. In one hand she held a cut crystal decanter full of amber liquid, and in the other a frosted silver bucket of ice.

The humid room chilled as Miss Lizzie resumed her seat, setting her prizes on the table in front of her. She produced a thin cigarillo from somewhere in her improbable costume, struck a safety match on the terracotta of the centerpiece flowerpot, and plumed blue-grey smoke toward the plaster medallioned ceiling.

Starting with the spirits of the dead rising from the Navy helicopters and continuing after his discharge from the service, Van Vierlans had long been visited by entities he had no name for, beings which darted along the limits of his peripheral vision. They never came into focus no matter what his level of concentration or the speed of his planned attempts at detection; they just skittered on the edges of his awareness. It happened when he was alone, starting at magic light when the sun canted between worlds, his beloved evening pouring in on shadow-purpled silks and arcing silver threads along the edges that defined the streets and city of Chicago. He'd grown up mostly disconnected from his own culture, with the reservations and the resources needed to visit them both out of reach. Deep in the city, away from anyone who could explain things to him or give him the teachings he would have needed to make sense of his life, he stumbled through these surreal encounters. He got used to the creatures, mostly, until they showed their faces. These were worrisome—but he had dog medicine he'd been born with that lived within him, medicine he knew would be passed onto any children he might ever have; that much, at least, he knew about the way of his people. It had saved him more times than he would ever know, let alone count. White folks liked to say dogs *knew*, but that was as far as they got, with no other way to explain it. Well, that was the medicine, and folks with it—they *knew*.

He was alone in his room one fall afternoon. Might have

been snorting a line or two. Definitely drinking a quart of beer, listening to hardcore—probably Amebix or Minor Threat, maybe Bad Brains—on his crappy record player that needed to have the needle changed, and thinking about what to do that night, while the light on the yellow walls went from pale lemon to rancid butter. He was smoking a Newport, looking out the window through the blinds and feeling for an ashtray as the pressure behind his eyes adjusted to the sun dipping lower in the sky, the cast of the room changing along with it. It was then that one of the inky black beings poured along the wall, barely outside his field of vision on the right-hand side, about a foot and a half tall. It stopped, hesitating just before it got to where he'd be able to fully see it. He took a swig off the bottle, holding the cigarette up and away from the sweating brown glass with his first and second fingers, and stared down the length of the bottle while twisting to his left and sitting down hard on the edge of the bed. This brought him face to face with the startled creature. Though caught, it recovered quickly and took advantage of the unavoidable opportunity to hold his gaze. The bottom half of its jet-black face split open into an even darker grin, a hundred translucent needle-sharp teeth framing a pit from which no light escaped at all. Its ruby eyes were faceted with ten thousand diamond-cut surfaces and the whip-thin, blood-red slashes of its eyebrows rose in amusement at his shocked and whitened face. He maintained a respectful but uneasy relationship with the entities

enjoy the peated burn of single malt freshly bloomed. They smiled at each other, settled back into the upholstered dining room chairs, took off those starched hats. Beryl reached under her apron and into her uniform skirt and shook a couple squares out of her pack onto the lace tablecloth. Pearl grabbed them up, lit them off the pewter candelabra, and handed one to Beryl. Miss Lizzie rolled her eyes and ashed her cigarillo in a coffee saucer. The women considered their smokes. No one talked for a while.

Finally, Delilah cleared her throat again. "We gonna talk now or what? Everyone payin' attention?"

"Mmmmhmmm." They nodded and flicked their smokes. "We're ready."

Miss Lizzie seemed uncomfortable but said: "Please, Delilah. Enlighten our guest."

The lightning seen earlier finally made itself heard as the thunders arrived in full orchestral glory. They were urging her to tell it, too. The chandeliers flickered; the candles guttered. Delilah smiled, and began.

Delilah hadn't always been Auntie Delilah, the rock, the anchor of some white woman's household. She had been her own woman, and before that, her own girl, her sense of self present from the first day she could remember being Nenge—that was her real name—much less Delilah. As a child she had lived on Dataw Island, her home unchanged from the time when her grandparents rebuilt their village after the bluecoats liberated it from the Confederate rebels.

Upon real emancipation, the families physically reconstituted the lives they had lived near Cape Mount back in Sierra Leone, placing their homes in the semicircle fashion which offered structure and protection, safety and strength. Her father and her father's father were Kamajor, respected hunters and warriors of the Mende people; her mother was a hereditary Halemo of the Sande leader society, a chief herself, and Delilah saw no reason not to carry on the tradition. The people in her village looked to her for advice, and as a young girl she was called on to settle disputes among her peers and even among children three and four years older than she was at the time. She would become a *sowie*, a social chief, at age thirteen. In her was stored the knowledge her people needed to remain a people. But here she was, stuck in America, running a household and saving this woman's name and property more times than she cared to remember.

Miss Lizzie coughed like she had inhaled a bug. Pearl laughed while Beryl stubbed out her smoke, shaking her head.

"Look. I'm not saying I'm not happy to be employed, and proud of what we've accomplished over the years, but this is not what I was born for, no matter how much life tells me it is," Delilah continued, voice clear and raised. "I had vastly different plans for what my life would look like at this point. This arrangement may be fine for you, but for me, for us—we're waiting on the next life."

When Delilah was fourteen years old, she'd met a ghost one afternoon while crossing a field on her way home from school. "Missus," she beamed, having been made to speak English in school all day—the school where they had been calling her Daisy. "What can I do for you today?"

The spirit stared at her, its silvered face cascading again and again down the front of its spectral garments, an old-fashioned blouse and dress that were clearly defined, even if the entity's form was not. When Delilah repeated herself in English, the ghost began to crackle and fade. She switched to Gullah and the spirit resolved itself. The cascading stopped, and the face of a young woman took shape. It told her she had to decide between serving a man and his household or serving her people. She quickly decided it would be no contest. She would dedicate her life to the people, as any chief should, even as she'd take whatever limited employment would allow her to stay among her people, rather than head north like so many others.

"But never tell them your real name, Nenge," the spirit said. "It's better to go about with a name the buckruh will accept, a name which will provoke no inquiry."

Nenge knew her Bible, knew the names in it and what they meant, how their stories infused them with meanings that most folks ambled right by in their day to day. She could choose the sort of name that suited her, and these foolish white folks from up North that worked as teachers at the school wouldn't think too hard about it. They only saw their pupils as souls to be saved, not as thinking beings. Her ceaseless reading reminded her how an old French bishop thought women like Delilah, Clytemnestra, and Lot's daughters were a pleasant sort of evil—honeycombs and poisons. Her sense of humor told her to choose one of their first names as her own. She decided she would be known as Delilah.

She knew, even then, that in this life she would be plenty sad, but not in the ordinary ways, and not for the lack of a man or children of her own on this plane.

"What is a man, anyway?" Delilah said. "Like grown-ass children, incapable of washing their clothes, or fixing their own meals, or finding a pen or an envelope, a spare button, or the place where they last left their reading glasses. Where is this, where is that, where is my church shirt, what time is the preacher visiting? Good lord, what drudgery and wastefulness it would have been, to spend a life tending to a man possessed of that dubious and unearned station *master of the house* and to raise his fool children."

Delilah cared about her people, doubtless, but preferred to do so on a broader scale—the business of marriage would be best left to her younger sisters, neither of whom had been given a traditional name. She had neither the temperament nor the patience to live any life except one that would see her in continuous conflict with authorities, social, legal, and cultural. She was, after all, the daughter of warriors and chiefs on both sides of her family. What would her ancestors think if she became a housewife?

"Yes, yes, Delilah. We all know of your 'royal lineage.'" Miss Lizzie made air quotes with her fingers. "And now our guest does as well. But tell him, if you would, of this foolish notion you have about Peter's creations. It would seem to be the dramatic conclusion of this story you're spinning."

Van Vierlans stood up, grabbed the sparkling decanter, and refilled everyone's glass. When he got to Miss Lizzie, she placed her hand over the top of her highball, but he was possessed of superb dark, dark blue eyes, and more than well-developed persuasive faculties. He met her gaze, tilted his head, and produced the suggestion of a smile, turning the light up in those orbs enough so she relented, and he poured generously, draining the last of the scotch in the leaded crystal into her glass. He grabbed the silver tongs from her bucket and dropped a couple of mostly melted cubes on top of the smoky liquid. She lifted the frosted glass and tilted it to her fine-lined mouth, drinking deeply, holding her cigarillo up and away from her body in an oddly delicate manner. He smiled and glanced around for a way to refill the decanter. Pearl caught his intent, excused herself, and headed through the swinging door into the kitchen. He stood at the head of the table as everyone listened to the opening of the freezer, and the chucking of cubes on metal, along with some creaking cupboard doors followed by the clinking of glass. She breezed back soon after with a fresh ice bucket in the crook of her left arm, the hand of which held a brand-new bottle of Johnnie Walker Blue (in place of the single malt they'd been drinking up to now), angled down so the heel of her right hand could give it a solid crack on the ass. He grinned as she popped the seal and set the scotch on the table. God, he loved money sometimes, even if those who had it didn't know how to use it. He lit another smoke and settled back into his chair, eager for Delilah to continue her story. He flashed her the full top row of his teeth. She winked and cleared her throat.

"Mas' Peter, 'e duh—"

"English, please, Delilah," Miss Lizzie interrupted, loudly filling her glass with fresh cubes.

"Apologies, Elizabeth," she replied, smoothing her skirts. "Like I said before, Mister Peter returned to us from Princeton with a head full of ghosts. He was possessed by this idea he could create an army of robotic servants to replace us, replace the house staff." Delilah grimaced, emotion flushing her face. She used "mister" rather than the literal translation "master," and no one moved to correct her.

"And why was that?" Miss Lizzie urged.

"Like you said before, there are spaces here we would not—we could not—really, that no one should enter. And you can say what you want, Elizabeth, but we both know that—"

"That what? What?"

"I watch you move around here; watch you creak around the floorboards. And you don't seem all too comfortable to me. Seems like every step or so you take, there's a ghost groans right behind you. And you know it. I know you do."

Miss Lizzie tilted her head back, grabbed her glass, and drained it. As she set it back on the table and the ice cubes settled into place, she said, "Perhaps I know those ghosts, know them as my relatives."

"The pale in your face that's whiter than ever tells me otherwise," mocked Delilah. "And those robots he built and worked on obsessively—those *automatons* as you call them— you know those were ghosts, too, just on the inside. Mister Peter imprisoned the spirits of our people in them, made them do the work for free just like in the old times you all love so much."

Miss Lizzie looked as if one of those haunts were giving her a backrub just then. She reached for the decanter, filled her glass to the top, and swirled the Blue around in her hand for at least thirty seconds. She drank deeply, then glared around the table and said, "You've always been wrong about one thing, Delilah. The souls he used weren't Gullah. They were Indian."

The three sisters turned their heads to stare at their guest in unison.

The chorus roared in his ears. Ancestors young and old cried out, *unsimalayo, omakiyayo.*

Help us.

Warm from whisky, chilled from fear, he turned his watery gaze to the sisters.

Miss Lizzie smirked, her small victory straightening her spine in the high-backed chair.

One clock ticked and a second chimed out of tune as rain and hail pelted the windows.

No one spoke.

No one but the ancestors.

D ELILAH BROKE THE SILENCE. "Bullshit," she called. "Oonuh duh bad mout'—"

"Remember, Delilah, English, please. Let's ask the good doctor what he thinks about it," Miss Lizzie replied.

"Don't, Elizabeth," said Pearl.

Beryl lit another cigarette, sipped her drink, regarded the scene. "She's right. You ought to be quiet."

"I won't," hissed Miss Lizzie. "He knows what those circles represent, even if he wouldn't say so in his article. Isn't that right, *Doctor* Van Vierlans? Those stones represent the Guale who are buried there—thirteen in each circle, one each to represent our Savior's disciples and one for Jesus himself."

"You're talking crazy now, Elizabeth. Crazy, or whisky— it doesn't matter," said Delilah. "You're wrong. I don't know who the 'wally' are, but those are our people out there. They—"

"Are *not* yours," Miss Lizzie cut her off.

Delilah's mouth twisted. "But I read it in Mister Peter's journal. He wrote *Gullah*—I saw it myself."

"This one?" Miss Lizzie reached into the wall of books and pulled out a small, cracked, maroon leather journal with an insignia in flaking gold leaf at the bottom right corner. He made out a decayed "PM."

"You may have read it in his substandard penmanship, but you never heard him speak it. You would've known right away if he did because what he wrote was *Guale*. Here—see for yourself." Miss Lizzie offered the little tome.

Delilah snatched it out of her hand. Pearl and Beryl got up and stood over her shoulder as she turned the pages. Apparently, they had read it before tonight as well.

Delilah flipped through the pages. She soon found the passage and read aloud:

> *With a troop of our most trusted hands, armed to the teeth, we fanned out into the brush, driving the Guale before us. They were dispatched with as much mercy as we might show. When all were silenced, we began the grim yet glorious work of placing them as the Lord might want. So to honor his disciples, we placed and buried the heathens, marking their eternal rest with the painted white stones left in those places of power by the previous savage masters of the island. As our spades turned the last of the dust, I knew our profits to be ensured by the*

Heavenly Father himself. We had tamed a land and its people, as instructed in Genesis.

The sisters three turned their eyes but not their faces to Van Vierlans. Miss Lizzie licked and lit another cigarillo.

GROWING UP NATIVE IN CHICAGO, removed at a young age even from the neighborhood that kept Urban Indians sane, or at least together, Van Vierlans had struggled to maintain his identity. He'd stomped around the streets as a teenager, quoted Vine Deloria, gone to any powwow he could find, and learned his language and culture in bits and pieces from TV, the movies, cousins on the bus, scrawl on the El, the occasional newspaper article, and whispers in dreams. When the thunder beings visited him, the best he could muster for an explanation was Wolfen, or too much dope. Ancestors' voices crowded in but took their place in line with the howlers and the catechists.

Then it turned out the only way to escape the gang holding him in a place that would eventually kill or incarcerate him—not very different outcomes, he thought—was the military option two Gang Intelligence detectives offered him. "Four in the service or three to five in Joliet." And it was "♫Anchors away, my boys, anchors away♫."

Eight months later in Beirut, the days and nights were filled with twenty-four-hour-a-day flight deck operations.

He worked twelve- to fourteen-hour night shifts, tried to sleep and take one day at a time. But he bunked near the fantail of the O3 level, right below the flight deck. The birds turned up continuously, flying missions over a city gripped by a civil war which respected no one's time limits. He slept an hour or two here and there, the pillow and blanket he'd brought from home wrapped around his face in a futile attempt to drown out the 140 or so decibels produced by the exhaust of F-14 Tomcats and A-6 Intruders and AWACs and EA-6Bs and S-3A Viking Sub Hunters and A-7 Corsairs, all continuously searching and filming and buzzing the beach, employing the carrier's catapults and arresting gear without end. Sometimes he cried in frustration and sometimes he chewed the Sudafed he talked the corpsmen into giving him and passed out for what seemed like a minute at a time, that small relief keeping him mostly sane.

Where his shipmates kept pictures of their wives and girlfriends on their locker doors, he had a newspaper clipping of Dennis Banks on the run and receiving sanctuary from California Governor Jerry Brown, along with a color page torn from someone's *Hustler* of Russell Means when he ran as Vice President along with Larry Flynt for the man in charge. Who the fuck are these guys? his shipmates would ask. He'd reply, Do you really want to know? 'Cause this'll take a minute.

They were never interested enough to stick around.

His only buddy who knew who they were was from the Wind River rez. Vern. They both tried out for UDT/SEALS, anything to get off that fucking boat, running around the flight deck in boondockers, making the cut. Van Vierlans was a shit swimmer, said he'd go for the airborne thing though, would do EOD, but he got out of the Navy before he could start the training. Vern went SEALS all the way. Van Vierlans wondered about him still, knew at least that he wasn't one of the guys lost on the wrong shore in Grenada.

And that time trying to sleep through the shrieking from the flight deck? It was nothing compared to the ancestors howling in his head right now.

Miss Lizzie saw it first, smiled.

"Problem, Dr. Van Vierlans?"

His eyeballs settled like dice in a cartoon crapshoot. "No, ma'am. Not at all."

"That's good," she mused, taking a drag off her cigarillo. "We do care about our guests."

"I appreciate that, Miss Lizzie." He ran his fingers back across his hair, pulled on his ponytail. He glanced over at the ashtray, saw his American Spirit still burning there. He reached for it and said, "Can we visit these stones you seem so fond of?"

He felt Beryl kick Pearl under the table.

"I don't see why not, Doctor," said Miss Lizzie.

"Are you sure this is in the doctor's best interest, Elizabeth?" Delilah asked.

"Of course, *Nenge*." Miss Lizzie smirked. "Why wouldn't it be?"

Delilah paused, fast-licked her lips, searched her sisters' unsupportive faces, and replied, "Should be, Miss Lizzie. I suppose it could be a fine thing for the doctor to see."

Beryl didn't seem to think so. "Maybe we should wait until the morning. That way—"

Pearl cut her off. "I think we could go now. It would be fun."

B ERYL HAD BEEN the cautious one since they were children. Pearl, the younger sister, was forever jumping headfirst into whatever came their way. Some things never changed.

Back in the day, when Beryl and Pearl were still leely, *little*, and their mother more concerned with big sister Delilah than with them, the WPA came through, just as they had all over the country and particularly in the South. Here in Gullah Country, they were keen to reduce the swampland and keep some of the malaria in check; white folks who wanted to move in from upcountry on the mainland were susceptible in ways local folks were not. A lot of the projects depended on drainage systems, and culvert cutting was the quickest way to get them started.

These mostly whiteboys from the government weren't the most motivated gents Beryl and Pearl had seen work this area. The heat and the humidity got the best of them pretty early on in the morning, and accordingly, their equipment seemed to be strewn across the ground the rest of the day while they lay in whatever precious shade they could find. The two girls walked hand in hand one lazy afternoon, practicing their English and wondering at these men's inability to move in the blazing sun. Insects droned unseen in the bulrushes along the road. They laughed to each other about the alligators they imagined could rush up out of the ditches and feast on these lazy visitors to their homeland. As they rounded a bend in the road, they could see a broad dune covered in loblolly pine with a half-dozen rough-cut metal tubes lined up and ready for installation somewhere in the maze of swampy bottomland. One six-foot section leaned a bit over the lip of the hill, yawned in their direction.

"Let's go!" shouted Pearl, keeping with the English. She took off running.

"Where? What do you mean to do?" Beryl hollered, rolling her eyes.

Pearl slowed and turned. "You know, girl, I didn't need to see it to know you made that face. Let's roll down the hill!"

"You better quit, Pearl. Nothing good is coming out of that fool idea."

"Now don't be such a drag, Beryl! Let's have some fun!"

Beryl clucked her tongue. "Now, nothing, Pearl. You'll be lucky if you only tear your dress. Mama's gonna kick our butts for sure."

"Pssssst. You worry too much, sissy. Let's go!" She pulled at Beryl's hand.

Beryl rolled her eyes again. Couldn't hurt, she thought. Pearl's right. I hate being a drag, and it's been *such* a boring summer.

"Fine. But just one time, Pearl."

"Okay, okay! Let's go."

Beryl let herself be led across a short field. Pearl's eyes gleamed.

"Come on, sissy!" she squealed.

The two flatlander girls picked their way up the dune, exaggeratedly cautious in their steps.

"We made it!" shouted Pearl.

Beryl humphed. "Of course we did, Pearl. Jeeez."

"Don't you blaspheme," Pearl said.

"I didn't," Beryl replied. "'Jeeez' is not a blasphemy."

"It is too. If it ain't, go ahead and say it in front of Mama."

"You know I'm not gonna do that, Pearl."

"Well, knock it off. You're gonna give us a jinx or something."

"Fine. I quit it. Now what?"

"I don't know. Let's go for a ride."

"How we gonna do that, Pearl?"

"In this tube right here, girly. Ready?"

"Uh-uh. I'm not gettin' in that."

"Bock-bock-bock. Chicky-bock-bock."

"I ain't chicken. Take it back, Pearl."

"Shut up, Beryl. I'm sick of your shit."

Beryl's eyes opened wide. "Ooooooooh. You're in trouble now. I'm tellin' Ma!"

"You won't even," said Pearl. "'Cause if you do, I'll tell Mama you were looking at that boy Henry."

"No you won't!"

"I will. Try me!"

"I'll kick your butt, Pearl! I'm the older one!"

"By two minutes! I'll beat your ass for at least that long!"

Beryl was outraged. "Fine, Pearl. Do whatever you want. I don't even care."

"I will, Beryl. Watch this!" And she marched right over to the lip-hanging culvert, slipped inside, and shoved at it with her slight shoulders. A few times.

It went over the side of the hill.

Pearl rolled and laughed. After a few seconds those laughs took on an edge as Pearl realized she was trapped inside a raw metal tube chock full of momentum and a sixty-five-pound girl.

The corrugated steel hit a rock embedded in the side of the hill and the reverb tossed Pearl around inside. She half spilled out as the tube swerved in the sand. One of its ragged edges caught halfway up her arm. The point barreled down and dragged through the warm glow of her young skin.

She screamed and fell out onto the ground.

HER BLOOD FOLLOWED right behind her, sprayed like a fountain, and clotted in the fine white sand.

Beryl ran over, this scene having played in her head a hundred times already.

"Pearl, Pearl! You're gonna be fine. I know it!" she yelled.

Pearl held her arm close to her chest, rocked in place. Blood rivered through her fingers.

"You don't know that, Beryl!" she yelled. "I'm gonna die here! This is such bullshit!"

Beryl stared at her for a second, shook her head, and burst out laughing.

"Now I know you're gonna be fine, sister!" she yelled.

She tore a strip off the bottom of her dress, wrapped and wrapped her sister's arm, clucked her tongue, and shook her head. Tough girl Pearl choked back some tears and beheld Beryl with a new kind of love.

Beryl beamed at her baby sister, happy to be a drag sometimes.

Beryl looked at Pearl across the tired, sweating glasses on the table. "I guess maybe we could go for a little walk," she said.

Pearl smiled back at her big sister. "Sounds good to me."

Now it was Delilah who was clearly distressed. "I don't want to. Let's wait 'til morning."

"It's suddenly stuffy in here," Miss Lizzie offered, "and the rain's quieted down. Why don't we head out for a bit and see what happens?"

Memories clawed at Van Vierlans as well. "That works for me."

They rose mostly as one, gathered cigarettes, finished drinks, and grabbed jackets against the clinging mist and cooling ocean air. Delilah shook her head, reminded them that dinner still sat in the kitchen.

"It's all cold now, anyway, Delilah," Miss Lizzie declared. She turned, not missing a beat: "Be a dear and grab that bottle for us, Doctor, if you would, sir."

"Consider it done, madame." He grinned, caught pouring one more splash into his glass. He set the Blue down and drained the drink, suspending the tumbler in midair as the last two cubes dropped into his mouth. He ground them with his molars as he stubbed out his cigarette, then picked up and cradled the bottle, making his way around the table and through to the kitchen where he stopped at the freezer to fill his tumbler with ice before joining the processional.

T HEY WALKED OUT the back door and into a world that now looked completely different. It was pitch black beyond the dim yellow glow cast by the porch light next to the enameled green door that shut abruptly behind them. He paused near the top of the stairs, moths dashing their brains out on the antique glass next to his head while mosquitoes a hundred yards off perked up at the scent of his fresh blood on the blowing wet wind. Hordes of suddenly audible sandflies raced screeching to find purchase on any scrap of his exposed flesh. What was earlier a friendly, if unusual, garden was now utterly alien, every cranny and angle menacingly dark and full of fallen Southern angels and debauched spirits that cried out for the company of his soul. His compatriots paid the ghosts no notice and carried on as if they saw nothing save home and welcome in the damp darkness. He shivered involuntarily, swigged a healthy belt of the Scotch, and toddled down the cedar planks, catching up with the company of women.

Lagging behind their lilting voices, he lit a cigarette. As he walked with the smoke in one hand, he dragged his other across the finely clipped boxwood hedge, feeling the warm rain that collected on the tiny green leaves. The odd collection of humans in front of him wavered in and out of definition through the mist. He recoiled in urban disgust as his hand encountered the slime of a garden slug, its sucker pad attaching to his middle finger. He flicked it away into the bushes, wiped his hand on his leg, and found that his chinos were already dank with cloying humidity. He marveled at why and how anybody had ever settled here; the air itself would drown any sane human.

His heart started racing, and he felt a sudden need to catch up to the group. It was their talking that did it. Not necessarily the talking, but his inability to see their faces while they did it, that was the problem. He was desperate to see faces when they talked, for to him the words could mean anything without the visual cues he needed to make sense of a language not his first.

He spent quite a bit of his time in bus and train stations and at bars just watching people talk, looking for the lies given away by incongruities between their faces and voices, the twitches and darts of eyes and muscles. When he caught the same deceptions in anonymous passersby, he scanned their faces to catch a glimpse of the mothers and fathers they descended from, telling himself the story of how these inadequate children had dashed their ancestors' hopes for one or another or any reason at all—those were moments that he relished. The fucked-up families he imagined in his mind entertained him, for no reason he could discern whatsoever, other than to think there must be something truly wrong with him, with his soul that fed from the distress of others.

Distress began to overwhelm him now, though, as he sped on through this garden of unearthly delights; the night-bloomed jasmine and softly spreading moonflowers glowing in the dark filled his nose with undreamed-of scents and dread. Quiet scurries in the undergrowth became scritching nails on coffinwood; beads of rainwater catching any available light became glowing eyes that mocked his passing. He doubled his hustle and caught up with the women.

"Do you remember when we buried King out here, Delilah?"

"I do indeed, Elizabeth. Do you remember how he died?"

"Of course I do. How could I forget?"

"Really? I thought you might have blocked it out," said Pearl.

"Though that likely would have been preferable, it's not something I could have done."

"Well," Beryl said, "it *was* quite a memorable day, I suppose."

"You are correct, Beryl. The killing of that deer was quite an occasion," Miss Lizzie said, using the ironic British sense of *quite*. "But the death of my beloved Labrador Retriever, which poor creature should have been nowhere near that fool's errand, was unforgivable. I'm not sure I ever did recover."

"Fuh true. It was a sad, sad day, Miss Lizzie," said Pearl.

"Thank you, Pearl. It truly was."

Van Vierlans pieced together the story as they talked. Miss Lizzie's father had got it in his head one Sunday after church that a proper hunt was in order, the sermon that day having been a reading from the first chapter of Genesis all the way through verse 31. He embraced verses 26 and 28 in particular and felt fully ready to subdue nature herself. He readied a party of his men and their dogs, mostly Walker coonhounds and assorted beagles. They rode out to blast away at whatever they might encounter. Of course, Miss Lizzie's pet Lab, King, ran after them with tail wagging and tongue lolling, like Labs everywhere are wont to do. In the fury of the hunt, her father managed to shoot both the last remaining white-tailed deer on the island and her dog King.

One of his men brought the doe back on his shoulders while he himself cradled his daughter's boon companion in his arms, looking for all the world like a supplicant on a Nazarene pilgrimage. But she had read his face very differently.

"Yes. I remember that day. And I remember forcing Father to dig that grave."

"Me too." Pearl shuddered.

Young Lizzie had stood in a driving rain that day, imperiously watching her father dig in the soupy mud as the dirt he piled on the sides of the grave kept running back into the hole. She didn't cry, and she never blinked. King lay at the side of his future forever home. Lizzie refused to allow his eyes to be closed. She figured they should both watch her father's labors.

"Took him a long time to dig the hole," Beryl said.

"Yes, it did." Delilah sucked her teeth.

"As was fitting," said Miss Lizzie.

They walked on through the garden. Van Vierlans was suddenly colder than he should have been.

He gazed over his shoulder, back to the house, in search of a bit of warmth or at least reassurance. It leered at him, twin amber eyes over the rear galley and the toothlike row of dimly lit kitchen windows. The porch light was out now, and moths strained at the haze of watery gold that caught the high spots of the wet flagstones and impassive statuary throughout the garden. He raised the bottle and drank deeply from the Blue.

Houses had character, lives and ghosts to contend with—too many demands on attention and emotion that he'd rather not impose on his own life. Even living in a rented house was still an adjustment for him after growing up in apartments. Calling the landlord, even if it took them forever to show, seemed the way to go. The deflected responsibility along with the accrued emotions of years of renters living in anonymity was reassuring, far less taxing than the woes of homeownership. He glanced back one more time at the perfect affirmation of his choice to rent in a Chicago high-rise and returned to the path at hand.

"Dr. Van Vierlans, I believe you have our bottle on your person?"

"I do, madame."

"Let's see it." Miss Lizzie paused at a marble statue that might have been a saint or the hand-carved personification of Agony: an alabaster face turned heavenward, the mist collecting in the corners of its blank eyes. She snatched the bottle from his hand and poured liberally into her highball, a pair of sad cubes rising on the rich liquid gold. She handed it back to him and said, "I appreciate your foresight, if not your methodology, sir."

"I thought you might, on both counts, madame."

"You gonna share that, cousin?" Delilah inquired.

"Of course, Auntie. My apologies." He tipped a generous offering into her almost-empty glass.

Pearl elbowed Beryl and they stepped forward too, tumblers outstretched.

He smiled and poured away.

"Tengky, cuz'n." Pearl winked.

"You are most welcome, madame," he replied, smiling and topping off his own drink.

Her eyes lingered on his face. He blushed and cast his own eyes downward, disconcerted by her beauty getting the best of his buzz. What the hell is wrong with me? he thought—feeling a little off-key but staring back. Their gazes locked, and he struggled to break away.

"So, ladies," he recovered. "Where to?"

Miss Lizzie tipped her highball longer than any veteran drinker he'd ever known and said, "A little ways further, Doctor. Not to worry."

And so he worried.

HE LOOKED TO THE SISTERS, the warmth of the scotch creeping up his spine, a dull roar building in his ears. Lightning still popped over the water that he could smell but not see. The breeze shifted across his face, blowing his hair this way and that, but he was now too drunk to bother containing it anymore. He chain-smoked at will, unrestrained by comportment or interiors. The lucky feeling from his earlier garden reflection returned, though he was too intoxicated to appreciate the strangeness of that fact and its timing. He thought he could hear the ancestors, but the whisky told him otherwise.

As they walked, and talked, and drank, he noticed they were meandering eastward, back toward the front of the property.

"Ladies, where are we headed?"

"To the circles, cousin. We told you that."

"But inland? Away from the water?" He had never considered their exact location.

"Of course. It's safer. The shore floods quite a bit around here."

Makes sense, he thought. For the circles to have survived this long, they would've necessarily been constructed away from the coastline. He knew that, should've known that. He could feel his mind fogging, drifting, but his body felt otherwise, felt more than fine. He took another healthy swig off the scotch.

They cleared the defined edges of the garden and hustled across an open field of what smelled like sweetgrass, the moon peeking out from behind quick-drifting clouds. He thought of that scene from *The Great Pumpkin*, and the four women ahead of him all looked like Lucy.

He could see the glow of the path to the road shining in moonlight off to the right, and then the old tabby church. The company talked low among themselves, all of them drunk now, English and Gullah clashing in the dark, laughter barking out over the heavy humid night air. A loud giggle with an edge settled off to his right and onto the old tabby church. His eyes landed on the broken mullions of a glassless window. A streak from the greying moon lit up a portion of the interior. The tabby of the walls, such a unique building material, appealed to his scholarly inclinations, but it was something else that drew him to the stark building. Even his dulled senses screamed there was more he needed to see. He broke off from trailing the party and crept toward it, drawn to the silvery blue illumination within.

The women stopped as a company.

"Hey cousin! Where you gwine?!"

He pressed on.

"Nothing over there to see!"

A sound he'd never heard in his life rose from within the deconsecrated church. A sort of...*keening*, would be the only way to describe it.

"Come back, cousin!"

He couldn't stop himself.

"This way!"

Laughter followed the command.

He stumbled to the window and peered inside, his eyes desperately trying to adjust to the gloom.

Once they did, he accused them of lying.

At the back wall of the sanctuary slumped a man who could've been eighty or a hundred and eighty. A husk of a man, in whom he saw everything the women's talk had hinted at: the banished husband who once dared ask Miss Lizzie for a divorce. Or—*and?*—the father, who built the automatons, who shot King: the monster of a father who had impregnated her. The fact that this wizened figure, given its age, could and would have been her husband *and* father slammed home. Repulsed and intrigued, he cursed his own scholar's need to know. Vertigo crept up his legs and he steadied himself, grabbing the rough-cut windowsill.

Both of the man's arms were chained to rings bored into the wall. He wore nothing but a ragged pair of colorless pants. His skin showed the abrasion of her eternal indifference, calicoed grey, brown, and white, patched with dirt and riven with sweat trails, all his supplications answered with casual cruelty. A pewter pot sat off to one side and his filthy feet lolled in piles of chicken bones and potato ends, their tiny red eyes visible even in the gloaming. The prisoner's head rolled; his eyes met Van Vierlans's and the wretch made a croaking noise. It sounded like the capacity for speech had long left him, along with his mental faculties. Van Vierlans found himself incapable of movement, unable to comprehend what he was seeing. Behind him, he could just make out the women giggling and chatting.

"Cousin. Don't concern yourself with all that!" one of them hollered.

His mind reeled. Not just at the *what* this creature was, but *who* he was. Every one of Miss Lizzie's cruel and callous glances rolled over his internal viewing screen.

He felt the footsteps behind him before he heard them.

Delilah placed a warm hand on his shoulder, let it sink in.

"Cousin, this really doesn't concern you. We need to explain the hoax of the circles to Elizabeth. Otherwise she'll never leave it be."

"I don't understand," he said, about a number of things. "What?"

"This, this thing. And the 'hoax' you're talking about."

"Okay. Which first?"

"Well, uh, this *thing* in the church would be a good start." He took a swig straight from the bottle, met her stare.

She returned his gaze and held her tumbler out to him. He poured, generously.

"It's like this, cousin. Mister Peter there—"

"Peter? Senior or Junior?"

"There's only one Peter."

"So, father and husband to Miss Lizzie?"

"We told you that, cousin. You don't listen."

He took another drink.

Listened.

"This family's never been quite right," she continued. "Always have done things their own way."

"But that's against the law. You can't—"

"They *are* the law out here. They own the whole island."

He lit a cigarette. Took a long drag, held it in, blew it out slow and pushed the hair off his face.

Sure, strange shit had happened in his neighborhood, growing up. Brothers and sisters, bad dads, kids sold for dope, it was there, and terrible. But father-daughter marriage? That was some ancient-Egypt-level weird. And this chained-in-the-church scene took it one step beyond. He suddenly found himself a little tired and a lot drunk. He hit the bottle again.

Delilah drank, too, and smiled at him over her glass. "Whatcha thinking about, cousin?"

He sighed, "Nothing."

"Hmmm. I'm not so sure about that." She took her hand from his shoulder.

He turned around. "Delilah, why the hell am I here?"

The rest of the ladies had inched closer. They were listening now, not talking anymore.

"Why do you think, cousin?"

"I just came down here to give a talk tomorrow about—"

Delilah laughed, a little too loud. "Oh, cousin. There's so much more to it."

"We need something you've brought," Pearl cut in.

Beryl smiled.

"Here, hand that to me." Miss Lizzie grabbed the bottle from him, poured, drank. "You could say it's to settle a bet, but that seems a bit crass. Let's walk some more."

"But what about your—uh, the, you know…"

"Him? Mister Peter?" she said.

"Yeah. What about him?"

"What about him?"

"Isn't his situation a bit inhuman?"

"His imprisonment in the old church helps him remember what he's done, maybe helps pay for what his family has done to all of us through the years," Pearl said. "The cruelty, the enslavement."

"Oh, Pearl. Don't be so dramatic," Miss Lizzie huffed.

"Elizabeth, really," Delilah admonished.

Miss Lizzie glared at her. She raised her highball, then touched it to Delilah's tumbler. "Fine, fine. Pearl is correct. It's a punishment we've all agreed upon for his many crimes."

"But what about him? How does he feel about it?"

"He's a monster, Doctor. As they say, who gives a fuck?"

"But he was your husband."

"*And my father.*"

THEY MADE THEIR WAY BACK over to the sweetgrass field and headed toward the tree line. The purple-white moon hung heavy in the humid sky to their left as they headed south, its fuzzy glow picked up by the unseen water below. Thin blue lightning razored through the fog in random patterns, answered by low thunder. The water suspended in the air grabbed up whatever light the night could offer and held it in front of their misted faces. Beryl called for the bottle and filled her and Pearl's glasses. She handed him the bottle and he tilted it back, finished it off. Miss Lizzie rattled her cubes at him in disdain. Delilah magically produced another bottle of Blue from deep in her bag, slapped its bottom with the heel of her hand, and cracked the seal, laughing. Miss Lizzie chuckled. Beryl and Pearl held up their skirts against the damp of the grass, tightly gripping their tumblers all the while.

The incongruity and irony of the scene was not lost on him. This—to his mind, anyway—*plantation owner*; three Gullah women; and a Native professor. All drunkenly making their way through a dark Carolina island pine forest in the middle of a night chock full of lunacy. It would make for quite a story. A small part of him wished for a devastating tragedy just so he could watch from on high as some hick sheriff tried to explain it all in the future for an impassive and jaded audience.

"So, what is it you need from me, cousin?" he said to no one in particular.

"You'll see. Not to worry."

And so he worried.

But on they walked.

THEY SOON PASSED the tree line, shaggy-barked lob-lolly pines and forest-floor ferns dripping in dew and slow rain, rotted leaves and deep dark moss muffling their drunken footsteps. This timberland had a wholly different feeling from any he'd been in before. The forests of Maine were cold and empty but held no malice; the endless pines of Montana were mostly spiritless and quiet, needing only a passing acknowledgment. The hardwoods and ivies of Connecticut were malicious, full of little people who required gifts and offerings, or you'd soon find yourself lost. Weighted down with centuries of conflict and duplicity and evil dealings by colonials, which stained the trunks of ancient trees and made spiteful deadfalls that would snap your ankle for the joy or hell of it. Dark as it was, he toddled along behind the women who effortlessly knew the way.

They chatted among themselves in Gullah and English. Delilah's hand reached back out of the dark, holding tight to the Blue. He took it gratefully, drank deeply, full-body shuddering and breathing out of his nose. He held on to the bottle, took the opportunity to engage her in conversation, quickstepping to catch up and keep time with her.

"About this thing you need, Auntie. Can you say a little more?"

"You worry too much, cousin."

"Well, it would be good to know. I didn't bring much with me."

"It's okay. We need your *nephesh*. I imagine you have plenty of that, cousin."

"What?"

"I imagine you have plenty. Am I wrong?"

"Nephesh? Is that some kind of biblical shit?"

"You got it, cousin, but watch your tongue out here near the sacred circles. Your nephesh is your…soul, in essence. It *is* a biblical term. So you're right. It's a little more complicated, but that's the gist."

"I'm a little drunk, yeah, but how is that gonna happen?" he said, thinking how the old nephesh was already spoken for by Big Daddy Downstairs. Maybe they'd cut a deal with Him.

"Up to you. You can give it to us, or we're going to take it."

Jesus Christ, he thought. This is really happening to me. He tried to remember how much the honorarium was.

"Were you going to *talk* to me about this, or—"

"I'm talking to you about it now, cousin."

He took another drink, chuckled.

"Okay," he mumbled, his drunken self a little excited by the whole idea. Giving nephesh sounded decidedly dirty. "Why, Auntie?"

"We got a thing here we need to take care of."

"That's still a little vague, Auntie."

"You were there when Miss Lizzie read it. It was written in the old man's journal."

"And?"

"We didn't know why she had insisted on *you*. Now, we know. Now, we all agree."

"On what?"

"The circles, cousin. What they need."

"They're not even real shell rings. They can't be."

"The circles are all the same. Each one is a ring of twelve stones with a thirteenth in the middle. The circle we're headed to only ever had twelve. When Miss Lizzie made her daddy bury King in the middle of it, it was so he could be the peacemaker, keep everyone and everything in its place. Pearl thinks burying you there instead will heal the island. Free the ha'ants."

He shuddered. "Well, fuck that."

"That's what we said, cousin. But she insisted."

"You are *not* burying me out here for 500 bucks."

"We know. It's why we convinced her your nephesh would be sufficient."

"Jesus Christ, Delilah," Van Vierlans slurred.

"Don't blaspheme, cousin."

"Sorry."

"It's okay. It's good to be scared sometimes."

He took another deep pull off the scotch and lit a cigarette. Delilah kept pace with him, described the different trees and plants they passed. His nerves calmed and his mind turned over the whole *nephesh* thing. He was pretty good with words, but he'd never heard it before. His guesses as to its meaning were constantly shifting. Some were pleasant; some horrifying.

Delilah seemed to sense his thoughts. "You'll be fine, cousin. You're just kind of a heathen is all."

"We'll see, Auntie."

THEY CAUGHT UP with the rest of the group. Miss Lizzie inquired after the new bottle. He took a drink and handed it to her. She filled her glass to the lip, melting the few remaining cubes. Talk about blasphemy—scotch this good on the rocks was an abomination, but when in Rome. Beryl and Pearl topped off their tumblers. They handed the Blue to Delilah, who poured a modest shot into her glass, then tucked the bottle into her bag. They toasted one another.

"Well, Doctor. The ring is just beyond this stand of cedar," Miss Lizzie said.

"Is that right?"

"It is, Professor," said Pearl.

Delilah smiled at him, raised her glass.

"Let's have a look, then," he replied.

They cut through the copse of cedar, its cleansing breath settling behind them. He bounded over a clump of ferns. The clouds broke with a ball of amber lightning, illuminating twelve bone-white, flour-bag-sized burial stones arrayed in a perfect circle—inside of a far older, wider, traditional shell ring. A rotted wooden cross carved with the word *King* stood in the center. I'll be damned, he thought, so there is a shell ring after all. Someone had built a new circle within the ancient hoop, maybe hoping to capitalize on its existing power, or maybe merely for convenience's sake. In any instance, a low thrum seemed to vibrate the air between the two, and he squinted both eyes as his ears processed the roiling power.

Delilah produced a folding truncheon from that magic bag of hers and handed it to Miss Lizzie. "'E ya dawg, Missus. Oonuh da dig."

"Yes, I suppose," she replied, setting down her highball

and heading out to the center, shovel expanded and held over her right shoulder.

He set down his drink as well, shoved his hands deep in his pockets.

Beryl squatted down, sipped at her scotch.

Pearl held her tumbler in her left hand, reached across her flat stomach with her right, and held onto her hip.

Delilah folded her arms and watched.

MISS LIZZIE gently laid the handmade cross to the side and began to dig. The party sipped their drinks, no one speaking at all.

She made quick progress—the ground was soft with rain and fog—and dirt piled up to the right of the grave. She soon disappeared when bent over, which meant she'd dug down at least four feet, though no bones had appeared.

When the pit was so deep that she stood back up and only her head and shoulders showed, Delilah asked, "Miss Lizzie. Where's King?"

"I don't know, Nenge. But he's not here, that's for certain."

"That doesn't make any sense."

"You've got that right," Miss Lizzie replied.

Uneasily, Van Vierlans stood up and made his way over to the grave.

"See?" Miss Lizzie said. "Empty."

He sat down hard at the edge of the pit, pondering.

"It makes little sense, madame," he offered.

"Indeed."

Delilah and her sisters walked over, joined him around the grave.

"What does this mean, Miss Lizzie?" Beryl asked.

"I can't say I know," she answered.

For fuck's sake, he thought, drunker than he'd been in a long time. This is ridiculous.

Fatigue washed over him with a sense of urgency that felt like walking bedspins. He lay back on the ground, legs dangling into the open space, mind spooling into the dark and separating from his body for a time he couldn't comprehend or recapture.

Disorientation and drunkenness ebbed through his mind as it returned to his exhausted body. He fished in his pants for his lighter and lit a smoke. Found his glass in the grass and drank deeply, the whisky warm and fragrant. He held it along with his cigarette in his left hand, the smoke rising in the quiet, still air. He tapped out finger exercises with his right hand. He thrummed his thumb across the tips of all four, finishing the imaginary guitar lick as a rumble of thunder started out low, then built in volume.

Lightning flashed through the grove around them, illuminating the scene, strobing their searching faces in slow motion. The wind picked up, sighing through the pines. The smoke in his hand no longer rose straight up, encircling his head. He took a last drag off the cigarette and flicked the cherry into the grave, then rolled the remaining tobacco out as the redlight sizzled in a puddle of crypt water. He got to his feet, unsteady, and shoved the butt in his back pocket.

Beryl jumped up and shoved him hard into the grave.

He reached out for the far edge, missed, and landed on his face in the damp hole.

"Hey! What the fuck?"

Clods of sod and mud immediately began to drop on his back. The women furiously pushed piles of dirt onto him from the side of the pit, Miss Lizzie plunging her shovel again and again. The mound began to weigh on him as he struggled to turn over. Exhaustion and liquor worked hard to defeat his efforts. When he finally flipped onto his back, the four women at the top of the hole were backlit in the lilac glow from the lightning crackling all around them, their grins wide and malice-filled, eyes glazed in silvered distance from their humanity. Thunder and the rush of blood filled his ears, drowning out their laughter.

The dirt was relentless, pulling him back even as it pushed him down deeper.

Tunkasila. Unsimalayo. Wocikiye...wocikiye. Omakiyayo... Wopila tanka tunkasila...unsimalayo... Wani waciyelo ate. He heard himself say the words, praying.

Amazingly, he also heard them returned from above. Nowhere and everywhere, somewhere, the ancestors were with him in this moment. The realization brought him peace. If they had appeared to him, then they had indeed been freed.

But so had the dogs the women off-handedly warned about earlier.

Deep in his chest, he felt the Morning Star's hounds burst through the dual panes at the front of the house—that lying fucker—imagined the shattering of glass singing in his ears as they tore through the Tiffany lamps and baroque furniture and out the back door. They skittered and found purchase on the wet flagstones, where they joined their ghostly local brothers and sisters, then bounded over the sweetgrass fields, slashed through the cedar forest, and burst into the glade where the women were burying him alive.

He heard their white teeth tear into the sisters' backstraps and hamstrings even as his heart burst in his chest. His eyes gazed up with fading light as King was reunited with his mistress, his jagged teeth sinking deep into the lacy crepe of her purple-veined throat.

A snatch of nightmare long forgotten came to him as his last breaths plumed into the fury above, a vision from deep in his youth.

The woman he now knew as Nenge had yelled at him—in the nightmare long ago just as she had when they first met tonight, though he didn't listen either time:

"Dainja! Mek straight'n fuh de do! Mek'ace!" *Danger! Run for the door. Hurry!* "Git 'way f'um yuh!" *Get away from here!*

He hollered back,

"Uh gwin'!"

I'm going.

ACKNOWLEDGMENTS

I'd like to thank the faculty, staff, and community of the Gullah Studies Institute and the Penn Center in St. Helena Island, especially Aunt Pearlie Sue. You do amazing things in an extraordinary place, and I count my time spent there as some of my most memorable and significant days. Many thanks to Mackenzie Cory for your assistance in putting this story out in the world the way it needed to be. Thanks as well to ever-generous Stephen Graham Jones for the read and notes. To Christine Neulieb for your editorial guidance and assistance, and all the fine folks at Lanternfish Press— I'm so glad for the chances you take.

ABOUT THE AUTHOR

Theodore C. Van Alst, Jr. (enrolled Mackinac Bands
of Chippewa and Ottawa Indians) is the author of
award-winning mosaic novels *Sacred Smokes* and *Sacred City*
and the editor of *The Faster Redder Road: The Best UnAmerican
Stories of Stephen Graham Jones.* He is the co-editor (with
Shane Hawk) of the Vintage/Penguin Random House
bestseller *Never Whistle at Night: An Indigenous Dark Fiction
Anthology.* His work has appeared in *Southwest Review, The
Rumpus, Chicago Review, The Journal of Working-Class Studies,
Apex Magazine, Red Earth Review, Indian Country Today, Great
Plains Quarterly*, and elsewhere. He is an active HWA mem-
ber. Find him online across platforms: @TVAyyyy